P9-AGI-957

State of Siege

RENEWALS 458-4574
DATE DUE

WITHDRAWN
UTSA Libraries

State of Siege

Juan Goytisolo

Translated from the Spanish by Helen Lane

City Lights Books
San Francisco

El sitio de los sitios © 1995 by Juan Goytisolo
English translation by Helen Lane © 2002 by City Lights Books
All rights reserved.
No part of this book may be reproduced, in any form, without written permission from the publisher.

Originally published as *El sitio de los sitios* by Alfaguara, Madrid, 1995
Published in the United States by City Lights Books, 2002

10 9 8 7 6 5 4 3 2 1

Cover photograph: Gradska Vijecnica, Sarajevo's national library in flames, Sarajevo, spring 1992, by Sahin Sisic. Copyright © 1992 by Sahin Sisic

Cover design: Stefan Gutermuth / doubleu-gee
Book design and typography: Small World Productions, San Francisco
Editor: Robert Sharrard

LIBRARY OF CONGRESS CATALOGING-IN-PUBLICATION DATA

Goytisolo, Juan.
    [Sitio de los sitios. English]
    State of seige / by Juan Goytisolo ; translated from the Spanish by Helen Lane.
        p. cm.
    ISBN 0-87286-406-5
        I. Title.

PQ6613.O79 S5813 2002
863'.64--dc21

                                                                    2002067609

CITY LIGHTS BOOKS are edited by Lawrence Ferlinghetti and Nancy J. Peters and published at the City Lights Bookstore, 261 Columbus Avenue, San Francisco, California 94133.
www.citylights.com

Library
University of Texas
at San Antonio

To the inhabitants of Sarajevo who, caught in the rattrap, fought against the cowardice and indifference of the world.

To its intellectuals and writers, the honor and conscience of Europe.

To Susan Sontag, who brought me to the city.

Several voices speak in the poet:
Let us listen to their harmonious chorus,
In which the seemingly dominant voice
Is but one among the others.

LUIS CERNUDA

I. HYPOTHESIS CONCERNING "J. G."

Vision of Winter

Through the hole pierced in the plastic of the window—by stray shrapnel or by an inquisitive and claustrophobic guest—the traveler had been peeking out since dawn at the desolation of the landscape. He had fallen asleep instantly—in his leather jacket, his military trousers, and his fur-lined boots—as the candle burned down, forgotten, on the night table: his thermometer showed seven degrees Celsius. Not one whistle of a bullet, not one rattle of a machine gun, not one exploding shell: nothing but silence, disturbed every so often by the swift throbbing of the engine of a vehicle or of a white armored car.

He had arrived the evening before at that vast funereal pantheon bearing the name of a hotel. After filling out his registration card beneath the grim, glassy-eyed stare of the receptionist, he took the time to examine the crypt—scarcely visible in the insidious creeping shadows—whose outline reminded him of that of the skyscraper-cathedral that Gaudí had dreamed of building. Its deserted and icy central area, its stories like stacks of prison cells, the empty bar and easy chairs looked like sets and flies of a decrepit stage decor. The flickering light of the candles and the beams of the pocket flashlights brought to mind the roaming or wandering of souls in purgatory. Fireflies or will-o'-the-wisps? Nightmares or a Dantesque theatrical set? The darkness had flung itself with vulturelike avidity on the last redoubts of shadow. He went upstairs to the fifth floor, searched for his room number, practically feeling his way along, and entered the stygian shadow of his sepulcher. Dinner would be served an hour later in the dining room in exile on the mezzanine, but fatigue from the journey got the better of him. He collapsed on the bed with his cigarette lighter, thermometer, and candle, not even bothering to unpack his luggage.

The light awoke him: a sickly pallor that made the furniture in the room look incongruous and absurd. Useless lamps, an antiquated sofa and a pair of easy chairs, a glum still life hanging lopsided on the wall, drooping out of sheer depression. The candle had burned down and now formed a sort of crater in the ashtray. His hand that had stretched out to open his toilet kit and get out his toothbrush fell limply to his side. A sign at the reception desk warned hotel guests: no running water.

The transparent patch over the window cut him off from the outside world. He moved closer and discovered the hole in it. With his eye glued to it, he could take in all the space extending from Sniper Alley to the bullet-riddled, battered buildings along the former commercial artery. The light, though attenuated by the fog, little by little revealed the tortured face of the city.

He stood there, all eye—did the rest of his body still exist?—surveying the visual field afforded by the peephole as avidly as the condemned man drinking down the last swallows of his life. Softened by the rigors of winter, the landscape was impressed upon his mind with the sudden violence of a dream: tormented, foggy, unreal, its stumps and wounds covered by a vast, merciful shroud. Helplessness, loneliness, nakedness of a moving panorama of ruins, skeletal buildings, dismantled vehicles, charred streetcars, kiosks reduced to molten heaps, gaping holes, scrap metal, pathetic residues of the ravages of fire. The snow—millions and millions of snowflakes—rent the gusty air, dancing, as though to mask the magnitude of the crime with its innocence: a charitable carpet offered the victims or a guilty coverup by the aggressor? The entire length of the avenue decked in snow: nonexistent traffic, a few ghostly fleeing silhouettes, the armored personnel carriers—also white—of the International Mediation Force.

Was he witnessing—or participating in?—the gradual extinction, the slow consumption of objects, bodies, and souls? His own immateriality was summed up in what his gaze revealed: whiteness and devastation. In the shelter of the gloomy and careworn buildings of the Austrian era, little figures numbed with cold were moving about, an exhausted passerby was pushing a handcart, an old man, motionless as the statue of the Comendador, appeared to be pointing an accusing finger at the besiegers on the hilltops.

It was then that he caught sight of her: she had appeared at the street corner, a few meters away from the burned-out kiosk, the fatally wounded streetcars, the place where in the summer he had seen a young man fall, suddenly mowed down by the well-aimed bullet of a sniper. It was a woman's silhouette, dressed in a dark winter coat and her head covered with a kerchief. Impossible, at a distance, to determine her age: her slow pace could be attributed to old age, caution, or simply fatigue. She was carrying a little oilcloth bag in her hand: her meager store of supplies for the day. She had stopped to catch her breath before crossing the avenue and exposing herself to being shot by the men lying in wait in the blocks of houses on the other side of the river. She made a feeble gesture to hail an armored car passing by, but it continued its useless patrol along the avenue: no braking; just a lightning-quick acceleration, without a trace of commiseration.

The woman sought shelter among the walls of a ruined building. The route that she was about to take ran directly along the snipers' line of sight: a long sidewalk blanketed with snow, whose desolation stretched to the empty but beneficent shell of a charmless public building.

(Months later, he had consulted his anachronistic tourist guide to determine the original function of that charred structure: Parliament of the Republic or Museum of the Revolution?)

His gaze was riveted with unbearable anxiety on the minuscule, vulnerable, frail silhouette that gave the impression of hesitating or of marshaling its strength before starting down so perilous a path. As he had been able to verify on his visits to the morgue, the snipers had proved themselves to be thirsting for a particular sort of blood: that of women and children. An ordinary wall, scarcely a meter high, ran along the sidewalk, on the enemy side, separating it from what remained of a public garden or park, with carefully pruned trees: enough protection for a youngster making his way all hunched over, but enough for her? He held his breath, his face glued to the plastic patch over the window, when the remote little figure did something that disconcerted him: she fell to her knees. After a few interminable seconds, gnawed away by a thousand questions that he asked himself, he saw her begin moving along the little wall on her knees, like a penitent on Good Friday in the act of fulfilling a promise to Christ on the cross or a solemn vow of expiation.

He felt the pendular beats of his heart: a very fine thread joined him to the silhouette clinging to her bag, moving her torso with no visible lower extremities forward in the snow, in symbiosis with her, as though the two of them formed a single body. Had the hunters opposite her already spied her and were they perhaps awaiting a moment of carelessness when fatigue would cause her to straighten up and raise her head above the wall, so as to focus it in their sights and squeeze the trigger? He was sweating; despite the intense cold, he was sweating. Each centimeter gained by the woman on her knees kept him on tenterhooks. How to help her from his cell, a powerless Cyclops, reduced to a single widowed eye, consumed by anxiety? What sort of treasure was she lovingly safeguarding in her bag? Firewood, food, gifts for her four children? The snow was falling in oblique bursts, hitting against the plastic, wetting his eyelid. A figure fluttered about in his mind like a wayward, senseless snowflake. Four, had he written four? What secret bond had he established with that silhouette abandoned amid the winter desolation? Salvos of more shells, of bazooka fire, of rifle shots suddenly saluted, like a sinister reveille, the victims of the siege. The little figure halted and seemed to hunch over even farther, as a fearless driver raced down the avenue toward the defunct commercial artery. The din lasted several minutes: he and the crouching woman remained motionless, hearts pounding, waiting, the distance separating them miraculously abolished.

Helplessness, precariousness—of her, of him, of the world around them—were prolonged beyond the usual morning exercise of extermination. The city fell silent, its crippled buildings, their eye sockets empty, fell silent. How many human beings, hidden as he was, were waiting in the neighboring buildings for the wings of the Angel of Death to graze them?

The woman continued her Via Crucis. Sustained perhaps by the fact that she did not feel alone, having sensed the presence of an eye in the enormous bulk of the building with blind windows, sealed over with patches of plastic: that island or bunker in which each room was a columbarium, each floor a symmetrical superposition of tombstones. She had tenaciously covered half the distance, as though the prayers that within herself she addressed to God, to destiny, comforted her ears with all the warmth of emotion, of pain retained for so many years. Would she succeed in reaching the end unharmed? Would she be annihilated by a mortar shell or riddled by shrapnel from a fragmentation bomb? Would she escape the viciousness of the hidden snipers this time? Centimeter by centimeter—how to measure the anguish? —she reduced the distance separating her from the saving shelter ahead in the landscape covered with snow: schizophrenia, death's whiteness, oneiric immateriality, whirling snowflakes, an almost inaudible rustle of wings.

All of a sudden, everything exploded into a thousand pieces.

Report by the Major (I)

At 16:40 today, local time, the person in charge of civil matters concerning the International Mediation Force telephoned his superior to inform him that a Spanish citizen had been hit by a mortar shell in his room at the hotel H. I., located on the Voïvode Putnika, better known, at present as Sniper Alley. After contacting the Department of Foreign Affairs of the Presidential Ministry of the Interior—already informed of the incident by the management of that establishment, in which press and television reporters, diplomats passing through, and members of various nongovernmental organizations are ordinarily put up—I went to the motor pool with the intention of proceeding to verify the pertinent facts and carry out the necessary formalities. As I write these pages the city is still undergoing one of the heaviest bombardments of the siege: the presidential radio station issued an exceptional order forbidding the movement of all persons and vehicles in order not to add new victims to the eighteen counted in the course of the day at the morgue of the central hospital. Humanitarian airlifts have been suspended and a thick layer of snow has blanketed the deserted streets and avenues of the city.

The din of exploding shells and the rattle of machine guns did not let up during the drive to the hotel. As we braked to park next to the one small door allowing access to the hotel, despite the fact that the fog had lifted and the armored car is marked very clearly with the flag and the insignia of the International Mediation Force, the vehicle was hit by a bullet presumably fired by the snipers posted on the other side of the river. I took cover from them behind the walls of one of the restaurants closed since the beginning of the siege, and presented myself with two junior members of my staff at the reception desk, located at the far end of the hotel's huge empty lobby. The light was beginning to fade and we had to use our pocket flashlights as we waited for the generator to be started up. According to the information given me by the acting manager, between 8:30 and 9:00 A.M. the hotel was hit by three rounds of mortar fire, one of which landed on the main façade, unoccupied for months; another in the former gaming room, likewise closed; a third on the fifth floor, on the right front side of the building, in the room in which our compatriot was staying.

I went upstairs to the aforementioned floor with my junior officers and two hotel employees and immediately located—there was a hole in the wall and debris—the room in which the shell had exploded. The walls were full of cracks; items of furniture, pictures, and lamps had been shattered and lay in pieces all over the floor. The corpse, presumably covered with the bedspread, lay at the foot of the sofa. I write "presumably" because on pulling away the spread to identify the body I noted to my surprise that it had disappeared. The hotel employees seemed to be as bewildered as I was. They themselves had covered it after the visit of the medical examiner and the filling out of the death certificate as they waited for the arrival of the ambulance, thus far postponed by the aforementioned order forbidding traffic to circulate through the city. The astonishment and consternation of the personnel from whom I took statements with the aid of the acting manager—statements that, together with the death certificate and other proofs concerning the incident will have to be handed over to the certified translators of our embassy in Z.—were obviously genuine: a death certificate without a corpse is not an everyday occurrence even in this country abandoned by the hand of God. As they tried to clear up the mystery by consulting the guard posted at the door, the concierge, and the remainder of the meager staff on duty, I made an inventory of the objects and appurtenances belonging to the man who had died, or rather, disappeared.

A candle burned halfway down and another spare one.

A flashlight.

A toilet kit.

A pair of fur-lined boots.

A military-style bulletproof vest.

A notebook with a green cover containing half a dozen poems.

A medium-size beige suitcase.

The contents of the latter have been listed on a separate sheet. They consist of two changes of underwear, socks, wool undershirts and underpants, and a ski mask, as well as several typed manuscripts written in our language, as were the poems in the notebook. The aforementioned belongings are now under lock and key in my office at the high command of the International Mediation Force.

The investigations of the hotel personnel concerning the disappearance of the body had led nowhere. No one understands how he could have been whisked away without attracting the attention of the guards posted around the clock at the service door. The consultation by telephone with the hospital morgue of K. add to the mystery. No foreigner is listed among the day's victims.

But what added the crowning touch to our perplexity was my investigation later on at the reception desk: his passport had also disappeared! The clerk at the desk, her face ashen with fear, swore repeatedly that she had put it in pigeonhole number 435, that is to say, the number of the room destroyed by mortar fire. Although she went through all the drawers underneath the counter and the cabinet in which guests' registration cards are kept, her careful search did not turn it up. The possibility that it had been stolen, though categorically denied both by her and by the cashier, ought not to be rejected. The traffic in lifted and doctored passports is apparently flourishing in this city that has been besieged for twenty months now and the majority of whose inhabitants are desperate to escape. According to confidential reports that have reached our headquarters, the price of a fake passport reaches sums that are astronomical if one takes into account the lack of money and general poverty that reign in this human rattrap in which old well-off families keep warm by burning their period furniture and sell their jewelry so as to buy food on the black market. Unfortunately, the humanitarian aid we distribute does not cover the minimum number of calories necessary per day, and a liter of cooking oil, to cite an example, sells on the street for forty marks.

In view of the urgency of this case, I am writing this report so as to hand it over to the French lieutenant colonel, L. M., who is traveling overland to Z. tomorrow with a guarantee of his safety from the belligerents. The use of a fax machine and other usual means of communication seems inadvisable to me in a matter of this sort. We must avoid at all costs speculations and commentaries from the press that are to the detriment of the credit and prestige of our multinational command. Tomorrow I shall continue my investigation along with a functionary of the Presidential Ministry of the Interior, who has already been informed of what has happened. I for my part am going to proceed to read and classify the typed texts and poems, trusting that they will shed light on the identity of the man who has died—or disappeared—and the reasons for his journey to the Republic at the obvious risk of his life. After the brief year-end truce and the ephemeral visit of celebrities of the political, artistic, and intellectual world favorable to the government of the Republic, there are barely half a dozen journalists and correspondents still staying on at the hotel. In the last four days, when the airlift was still in operation, only three passengers with press passes signed up for one or another of the flights; but none of them was Spanish and none answered the description of the man in question, an individual, according to the hotel staff, about sixty years old, dressed in a green leather jacket.

I am taking advantage of this opportunity to notify all of you that the envelope with the wax seal of the Ministry of Foreign Affairs transmitted via Z. was personally handed over to the representative of the long-suffering Sephardic community, Mr. D. K., in his office of the "Benevolensiya."

First Dream

Hymen, veil, length of fine silk?

In any case, light-textured, easy to pass through.

On crossing over to the other side you suddenly find yourself at the foot of a familiar staircase: the one that you descended in your regular visits to the *hamam*, in your years of vigor and vitality, of youth forever gone.

Everything is still the same: the seats on the side upholstered in worn red plastic, Second Empire gas lamps, frescoes with Oriental motifs, zenithal light filtered through the skylight.

From her throne behind the minibar, Madame—pale, cadaverous skin; flame-red wig of an Amazon—contemplates the empty salon, abandoned by her cohort of gallants and customers in senator's togas.

Someone is playing the piano in the apartments upstairs, a melancholy piece, steeped in nostalgia, which moves you as you listen. Is it a Brahms sonata?

I didn't think I'd find you here, you tell her. Your establishment had a sign: Closed on account of death.

A few sick clients spread that malicious rumor, she says. As a matter of fact, I haven't budged from here.

Didn't you die during the epidemic?

Those incidents no longer affect either one of us. Why rake up the past?

I'm trying to remember the last time I set foot in your domains.

Time doesn't go by for people like us. No calendars, no watches! A person gradually gets used to doing without them!

You haven't changed. It seems like yesterday that I last saw you.

Yesterday, today, tomorrow! Forget those words once and for all! You haven't aged either.

Don't try to flatter me. The years don't go by without leaving their mark.

Look in this mirror here! You'll see yourself just as you were when you first came here accompanied by your ferocious body-guard. That big rough, tough man with a mustache like a pair of handlebars or a coiled whip filled us with a holy terror and a corrosive jealousy. He came down the stairs behind you and the sight of him electrified us. All my regulars were dying of envy of you; they raved on and on about his vigor and fierce appearance, they had heated debates about the length of his tool. They would wait for the two of you to undress and go upstairs to the floor with the lockup so as to glue an eye to the keyhole and take their pleasure spying on you. Or else one or another of them would give you her cell so that they could contemplate the two of you with me to their heart's content, thanks to the indiscretion of a mirror that allows a person to observe intimate secrets without being seen. Sometimes, in moments of solitude, I wander about in search of a ray of light and enjoy witnessing the furious contest between your closely entwined bodies. If it appeals to you to see yourself going at it hot and heavy, forgive me that crude phrase, you have only to come upstairs with me.

To see myself?

Yes, to see yourself. Follow me past the showers and the pool, up the spiral staircase, along the hallways with their faded paint. Can't you make out my customers in togas gliding away into the shadows, like creatures that flee the light? Keep your eyes peeled: you'll catch a glimpse of them there, under cover of the darkness, recalling moments of happiness and fulfillment, the attributes and talents of their proud gallants! Each little cell that you set foot in still bears the traces of your visit! Come on, crouch down and spy through this keyhole! Don't you recognize that strapping lad with his dressing gown open, displaying his crude equipment, inviting you to polish it and shape it?

He went back to his country centuries ago and I've never heard a word about him since!

Well, there he is right there with his arrogant ace of spades, spitting on the tip of it to lubricate it!

I don't even remember his name!

Everything is written down in my registration books. Date, hour, room number, first and last names, not to mention the video that will serve as proof on Judgment Day! Don't dally: other visions of glory await you! Do you remember your colleague in this cell?

I thought he was dead!

Just look at him, as alive and kicking as ever. With his heavy mace held high, the caliber of which my customers and I often estimated in our secret councils!

How is it possible for me to see myself in two different rooms at once?

You're in all the dungeons! In the one you saw, the one you're seeing, and the ones you're about to see! Have a look at this other bruiser! Wasn't he an occasional bodyguard of yours at one time?

I never came here with him! We met downstairs in a movie theater!

Abandon once and for all those burdensome concepts of time and space! Your eyes aren't deceiving you! Would you deny that that bayonet is his? You can't make an expert like myself believe you've forgotten it!

It wasn't in the *hamam*. The scene took place in the pissoir on Barbès!

Visions are mobile. What happened there can be seen here. Wasn't it precisely the *mundus imaginalis* that interested you?

Let me look at him a while longer. I'd completely put him out of my mind!

I brought him here to refresh your memory, not for your enjoyment! Each door conceals a different image. The scabrous curriculum that earned you your doctorate!

(Madame tosses the strands of her wig with an impatient gesture. She is extremely pale: her blood appears to have mounted by capillary attraction to her flaming red hair dye.

The notes of the piano—Brahms, it is Brahms!—come from closer and closer at hand.)

Who is interpreting that sonata in your private apartments?

Forget the music and remember the past! You must have the details of your dossier clearly in mind if you want to confront your examiners with any hope of success!

(Her voice has abandoned its veneer of courtesy and becomes more and more high-pitched and hysterical in the empty rooms.)

Crouch down again and scrutinize the scene, the being lying humbly prostrate, absorbed in his devotions!

Me?

Yes, you!

And him?

Huge, curved torso, hard, bulging muscles closely overlapping, massive skull, rough, weathered face, a two-pronged mustache with handlebars curled upward!

You're mixing up different times and different people!

(She points to the keyhole of a different cell and you cannot help but obey.

The lewdness of the scene takes you completely aback.)

She (addressing you in the familiar form): he brandishes his palpitating stiffness; he castigates your devoutness with it! he condescendingly offers it to you to drink from; he belligerently shoves it down your wide-open gullet!

Hey, that's one of my own poems you're reading!

Everything here is only writing! What difference does it make whether or not they're your verses if you will be held to account for them once you reach the isthmus!

(The fog lying over the besieged city blurs the contours of things. The piano, the notes of the piano resound in your head. Where are you really? With your eye glued to the hole in the window overlooking Sniper Alley or to the keyhole of an *ergastulum* in the kingdom of subtle bodies?)

Prolegomena to a Siege

The symptoms had been accumulating for some time. He could see them every day in the course of his walks in that quarter of the city, like a sarcastic prelude to that new world order proclaimed by the gurus of power and banking: social and moral collapse; firings en masse; muffled explosions of rage; sporadic outbreaks of madness; proliferation of secret identities, sects, and bands; public prophecies of an imminent Apocalypse. The invisible hand that scribbled them with chalk or spray paint multiplied its encrypted warnings. Only those exegetes or passersby experienced in the interdisciplinary reading of the codes of mural language succeeded in getting to the bottom of the meaning of certain hieroglyphs and scrawls, the phrases in Urdu, Turkish, Bengali, Kurd, Arabic, or Tamazigh that covered the walls of the venerable bourgeois buildings or the blocks of public housing standing empty, doomed to be demolished within a short time by jackhammers. Unlike the posters that in bygone days glorified in Uralo-Altaic the revolutionary struggle of the Peruvian masses or the now-faded paeans of praise of long ago to the hermetic paradise of Albania, the new graffiti did not seem to emanate from any organized group or transmit any sort of watchword. They were individual messages, cynical or desperate, denouncing the marvelous benefits of the global marketplace—that masterfully orchestrated "New World Symphony"—cast in the form of the universal panacea of ultraliberal dogma: "To protect our national industry the national working class must be thrown out on the street!" "The right to fire a worker with a kick in the ass!" "This is where junkies hang one on!" "Free horse for all!" "Order your syringe online!" "Consult our Christmas gift catalog: a thousand and one ways to spread AIDS!"

The elderly gentleman who, two summers before, spent the entire day sitting on a bench across from the café where, with touching faith in the future, men out of a job and the poor of the *quartier* bet a few coins on the horse races at Longchamp taped live and then rebroadcast, had little by little lost his neat and elegant appearance. He was still sitting on the same bench, apparently listening to the groundswell of human voices and roars with which the customers crowded in front of the television set metaphysically spurred on—without electric currents or Hertzian waves—their favorite high-spirited steed, but he was now dressed in a threadbare jacket and pair of trousers and his salt-and-pepper beard was unshaven. A retiree whose pension wasn't enough to cover the cost of his food and rent? or one whom the minister who headed his department had deprived of his social security benefits in a bold and innovative budget cut, thereby receiving the plaudits of the media? Impossible to know: our hero confined himself to spying on him, slowing down once he spotted him on the bench or sitting on the ground now at the entrance to a shop closed on account of bankruptcy or the death of the owner and in whose grimy display window the melancholy sign read: "Total liquidation of stock: closing for good." He had begun to descend, like many others, the irreversible slope of deterioration: he stared into space all day long without even consulting, as he once had, the racing sheet with the daily winning numbers or the horoscope of the day, rummaged through the litter containers and garbage cans in search of miserable scraps. He no longer had a fixed abode and teamed up—inseparable from his cardboard packing carton, treated with as much care as a brilliant executive takes of his briefcase—with half a dozen beggars, habitués of portes cocheres and the ventilation grilles of the metro. One day he discovered himself sharing with them their cheap red wine; uniformly covered with broken blood vessels and rags now, nonrecyclable detritus in the circuit of productivity that would have to be deloused and shoved under the shower before being let go with a full stomach and a spare sandwich, free to seize whatever opportunity might come his way on the street, available to everyone, yes indeed, providing, of course, that he was enterprising and dynamic, possessed of a competitive spirit and a natural aptitude for doing well in a free-for-all, virtues he obviously did not have, thereby condemning himself to parasitism and marginalization. He saw him later, in free fall now, sleeping himself sober, belly up, alongside the construction shacks next to the post office on the boulevard. The leaves were beginning to turn yellow and curiosity and a deep apprehension made him wonder if the man who had one day been the elderly gentleman would survive the assaults and the rigors of winter.

He walked on down the sidewalk leading to the Porte Saint Denis: the movie theater had just closed too! The general economic crisis even affected pornography! Feeling disappointed, he contemplated the usual bunch of Africans throwing dice at the entrance to the metro: as always the hunk with the sculptured Grace Jones hairdo dominated the game with his radiant physical splendor. He tried not to let his gaze linger on him and turned to look at the Pakistanis gathered round their compatriot with his sandwich cart: white tunics, Islamist beards, coiled turbans! The natives looked at them wary and ill at ease, out of the corner of their eyes. Were they members of the terrorist International denounced by the media? Were they getting ready to blackmail people, make attempts on their lives? On the corner across the street, the statue of Saint Anthony with his little pig and his crook seemed lost in a strange and hostile environment. At his feet, a black had fainted and was lying unconscious on the ground, gasping for breath, his torso leaning sideways against the wall of a building. He hesitated for a moment trying to decide whether to go on his way or cross the street to help the black, but a girl reached his side first. Blonde, plain, angular, wearing a blouse and blue jeans, she leaned over him, full of solicitude. This mark of solidarity and compassion, in contrast to the lack of sensitivity of the crowd standing round, cheered him. Still under the lenitive effect of this first impression, and still not realizing what she was up to, he watched the swift movement of the supposed benefactress as she went through his pockets, rifling the ones in his shirt first and then the ones in his pants: coins, crumpled bills, a ball-point pen, that she helped herself to in the blink of an eye before repeating her invasion of his pants pockets, yanking off the medal or amulet around his neck, finishing the job of picking him clean with one last touch as graceful as it was unexpected. The baseball cap with a visor worn by her fallen victim to shield himself from the sun changed owners in a second. The girl clapped it on her head and disappeared in the crowd without so much as a look back at the body of the junkie she had just stripped clean with such masterful skill.

The scene took his breath away: had the insectlike indifference of the bystanders, connected individually via the ubiquitous universe of images to the propagandists of right thinking, belied the reality of this multifariousness, this motley mixture, this heterogeneity? Or was this the counterweight, the compensation of that?

His excitement of years past, when he roamed about the *quartier* with insatiable curiosity, hunting for sensations and adventure, had given way to a more pessimistic, starker premonition: the ghetto, the interethnic war between ghettos, with its brutality and tribalism, would replace the ideal conception of the *cives* as the crucible of cultures. He crossed the street and went past the very spot in front of the Afro beauty shop where he had been graced one afternoon by an extraordinary vision: a dozen little African nuns, walking proudly back to the building that housed the Catholic Mission, had stopped and gone inside the beauty shop, only to come out moments later in an entirely different getup. Their svelte legs were showing, like flashes of glowing flesh, thanks to their daring miniskirts, and their perfectly coiffed bouffant hair reproduced the disconcerting alliance of gentleness and ferocity of the most popular model of *Vogue!* A hallucination or miracle that had obliged him to blink his eyes until he had persuaded himself of its prodigious destabilizing truth.

But the theophanies and illuminations had ceased, as if the

obligatory uniformity of appetites and desires excluded any sort of dissonance as a disturbing intrusion upon the diffuse domain of thought. The various ethnic groups of the *quartier* withdrew within themselves and appeared to be toughening up, to be regrouping their forces in preparation for possible confrontations and fateful clashes. Our character—let us call him that so as to identify him in some way, inasmuch as we do not know his name or what he looks like—noted, with a bitterness not entirely free of just a touch of pride, the imminence of the fulfillment of his predictions. Each day brought him further proofs which, although at first glance seemingly unconnected, nonetheless repeated, when seen from a broad enough perspective, the subtle pattern of the carpet as a whole.

On going down the stairs leading to the metro, he had witnessed inspections and searches as patrols armed to the teeth regularly went past in search of possible integrists and aliens without papers. The underground army of passengers strode ahead through the corridors with tense faces; the threatening clouds of the approaching storm gathered overhead. He suddenly spied a milling crowd of people moving away from someone, hurriedly and disgustedly leaving an empty space around him: an individual, a native of the country some forty years old, had let his trousers down, and with his posterior thrust slightly out was standing defecating for all he was worth. Filled with rage and Luciferian pride, he was pointing with one hand to his own excrement: yes, I'm shitting! take a good look at all this shit! it's mine and nobody else's! nobody can keep me from shitting! it's the one right I have left!

Our wretched hero trembled as he watched him. The man possessed by the devil, or a saint, hurled violent insults at the crowd, mingled abuse and great bursts of laughter: come on, come and see! here's the shit we live in! that's all there is behind their policies and speeches! shit, nothing but shit! The metro passengers assumed a dignified air, stepped up their pace, muttered scandalized comments: we've seen everything now, what nerve, doing his business in public! Walking in the opposite direction, the protagonist of our story endured as best he could the shoving and elbowing of those fleeing from the spectacle, the terrified and incredulous mass of those programmed for passivity and resigned acceptance of the law of the jungle, the consumers by proxy of the pleasures of others that were out of their reach, those knocked about without protest by the currents and spontaneous tides of the free market economy. Without falling into irrationality and dementia, how to rebel against the sage laws of nature?

Finally he felt that he was about to faint, unable to walk as far as the train platform, there to watch the scowling faces of the passengers as they tumbled out of the cars when the train opened its doors. His nocturnal vision had become reality: the Defecator was the wrathful prophet of his nightmares and his dreams!

The war, the siege, were about to begin.

Report by the Major (II)

To continue the previous report personally handed to Colonel L. M. to be delivered by him to our embassy in Z.: the following morning I presented myself with an escort and an interpreter at the Hotel H. I. where Captain Z. D. of the Presidential Ministry of the Interior was already waiting for us. The concierge, the receptionist, and the members of the staff whom I had interrogated the night before swore to the truth of their signed statements before the latter. According to them, our compatriot had appeared at the H. I. late in the afternoon of the preceding day and had handed over a Spanish passport, the name and number of which, through a regrettable oversight, was not recorded at the time in the daily guest register. No one saw him at the dinner hour in the dining room temporarily situated on the mezzanine, and it would appear that he did not leave the hotel or receive any visitors. He remained alone in room 435 and it was there that his life was unexpectedly ended at approximately 8:30 A.M. by the mortar shell.

I found the only new evidence concerning this unusual incident on the last page of the notebook of poems whose contents I shall offer an account of in a moment: the initials "J. G.," written by hand. But as I explained to the functionary from the Presidential Ministry of the Interior, these initials do not contribute a great deal to the solution of this puzzle. In our country, I told him, they belong to as many people as there are birds in the sky and fish in the sea: if one were to compile a list of all the José Gonzálezes in the land they alone would constitute a city the size of La Coruña. We went back up to the fifth floor to visit the room in ruins, taking advantage of the bright winter sunlight bestowing its diffident cordiality on this long-suffering city. We turned everything upside down, the furniture, the bed, the mattress, the rubble, in search of a clue, but to no avail. What troubled me most was the fact that there wasn't a trace of blood. The bedspread they had wrapped him in did not have a single stain on it anywhere; but how could anyone tell whether it was the same one that they had used to cover him? The hotel personnel swore that it was and when the medical examiner— Dr. F. K., who speaks fair English—arrived, he partially cleared up the mystery even though he did not solve the enigma. Our compatriot died of a heart attack brought on by the explosion. His body had only a few scratches and marks caused by the impact of its fall: it was probably hurtled against the wall some three or four meters away from the place where it had been. The medical examiner confirmed the sworn statements of the hotel employees: the corpse was that of a man of about sixty years of age, of average height and with thinning hair. He was wearing a jacket, a heavy wool pullover, and a green shirt that the doctor unbuttoned in order to auscultate him and see whether he had been hit by shrapnel. Informed of his subsequent disappearance by the presidential medical bureau, the doctor went that very morning, according to what he said, to the morgue in order to make certain that he was not listed with a presumed name among those who were waiting their turn for a fortuitous and furtive burial. The clerk who keeps the register states that among those admitted the night before there is no unidentified individual answering the description provided by the doctor: only an eight-year-old child, riddled with shrapnel in the street when a grenade exploded, whose body was recognized at the last minute by a relative, since his father and mother and brothers and sisters had already died during the siege.

I regret that the investigation has gotten no further and has not succeeded in unraveling this complicated episode: an anonymous corpse that suddenly vanished. In the present phase of the investigation all hypotheses are plausible. My colleagues in the multinational command with whom I have discussed the case at the officers' mess point to a possible connection of the victim with the local mafia, which specializes in various criminal activities such as drug dealing, smuggling, illegal currency transfers, and so forth. But, without definitely setting aside such a conjecture, I believe that the reading of the manuscripts found in the suitcase suggests other leads to follow.

A mere glance at the poems of the enigmatic "J. G." clearly reveals that we are dealing with an invert. The verses, of whose possible esthetic value I make no judgment, consist of a series of images and acts that, under cover of a cunning and sibylline language, constitute a shameless apology for vice. The abominable love, the love against nature, is presented, and worse still, exalted, in a crude and explicit manner. The title, *Sotadic Zone*, must be read as a complicitous wink in the direction of the celebrated English explorer and erotomane Sir Richard Burton, whose life and miracles were put before the public in our homeland by the author of *Forbidden Territory*. Not even in the most daring collections of poems by our decadent and languid bards had I ever read anything as vile, degrading, and disgraceful.

With this evidence in hand, the problem that now lies before us is why and how such an individual came to a city in which a person's life is in constant danger. S. is not exactly the most appropriate place for sexual tourism and a search for exciting amatory affairs. I confess that such a dichotomy—in the event that the verses are the work of the individual now dead and disappeared—is extremely troubling to me. There are too many contradictory and inexplicable elements in what, were it not a grievously real fact, I would characterize as an arcane mystery or a vulgar riddle.

I shall wait until I go on duty at the airport—the humanitarian flights suspended for the last forty-eight hours will be resumed tomorrow, if there are no unforeseen developments—to examine the remainder of the manuscripts of the deceased. Perhaps I shall find in them a piece of information that will help to clear up this murky affair. I shall likewise check to see in situ whether a Spanish citizen answering his description traveled during the last two weeks on a flight of what we have ironically named Maybe Airlines. I emphasize the fact that for the time being the maximum discretion and caution must be the order of the day. The prestige of our mission is at stake. Prowling about this strife-torn country are any number of Samaritans with press credentials who, beneath the cloak of humanitarianism and solidarity with the victims, make the most of the least mistake on our part to denounce our activities, to accuse us of complicity with the besiegers, and to depict the role played in the field by the International Mediation Force in the darkest of colors.

I await confirmation by telephone of the safe delivery of the documentation concerning this case to our embassy in Z.

The Defecator

The skinny little kid sitting on the curb at the foot of the monumental gate erected in honor of Louis le Grand was breathing in the fumes from the rag soaked in glue with a delicacy and languor identical to those with which the heroine of *La Dame aux Camélias* hid from her lovers her fits of coughing and hemoptysis with a fine linen handkerchief. The colorful group of youngsters with Afros was not in its usual place: had they taken refuge in a safe place or fallen into the meshes of a police dragnet? Uncontainable rumors had it that there was going to be a "Kristallnaght," directed against foreigners. The barricades around the public works site and spaces cordoned off on the boulevard around the post office intrigued a number of passersby and led them to express themselves freely. They're already set up for the Great Cleansing! a man in a beret exclaimed, in the tone of voice of an insider in the know. On the appointed day they'll round them up here before sending them back parcel post to the countries they came from! The passersby listened to him in silence and some of them nodded: yes, you're right, things have gone too far! If the authorities don't step in, we'll have to act on our own: take justice in our own hands!

The *quartier* was teeming with foreigners. A number of illegal immigrants, with scarfs over their faces to mask their identity, were getting ready for a demonstration. Our wretched hero was proud to discover among them the brawny young man he usually saw playing dice next to the entrance to the metro, with his athlete's biceps and his sculptured Grace Jones hairdo. He now had a red band around his forehead and appeared to be the leader of the gang of rebels. He wanted to speak with him, offer him his services, infiltrate the defense committees of the autochthons and pass on to him in secret their reports and plans. As he hesitated to step forward, someone suddenly grabbed him by the arm, and on turning around to see who it was, his face darkened.

They're all fundamentalists! the woman who lived next door to him said, pointing her finger at a group of Pakistanis. Can't you tell by their beards? They're plotting an attack or a killing in the neighborhood. What do they wear those long robes for if not to hide their weapons? On television yesterday I saw the arsenal captured by the police in the flat of one of them: machine guns, sawed-off shotguns, Korans, sticks of dynamite! People say they want to make women wear veils and those who refuse to will be raped and have their throats slit!

He advised her to calm down a little. He was certain that no one was going to force her to cover up the masterpiece constructed by her hairdresser, much less rape her with a will.

I hardly dare go out on the street! she sobbed. In the line at the bakery shop there were a bunch of bearded men with eyes like scorpions! One of them was wearing dark glasses like that blind imam who planted bombs in New York skyscrapers! I've heard tell that if his wives always seem to be pregnant, it's really because they're carrying explosives fastened to their sashes under their skirts and are getting ready to commit suicide attacks!

He calmed her as best he could and rid himself of her by lying to her, promising that he'd come visit her at her apartment at the hour when she was in the habit of drinking a finger of whisky in memory of her deceased husband. But meanwhile the athlete and his gang had disappeared.

The sidewalks of the Rue du Faubourg Saint Denis were crowded with beggars, as tattered and filthy as the actors in *Mother Courage:* they had stowed their pitiful belongings in plastic shopping bags from the Gap, Marks & Spencer, and the Galeries Lafayette as though they were inveterate customers of these department stores, and appeared to be advertising marvelous special bargain offers. The metro Defecator, dressed like the social agitators of the early years of the century as shown in the pages of *L'Illustration,* was haranguing them from atop a pile of empty fruit crates beneath a placard with an urgent cry for help:

WE ARE A SPECIES ON THE VERGE OF EXTINCTION!

His address was directed, as he proclaimed with the aid of a megaphone, to the unemployed, to the excluded, and to those booted out onto the street with a kick in the ass after years and years of faithful and loyal service by the brand-new doctrines of decentralization and flexibility of the workforce; to the victims of the scientific dogma of monetarism, the global marketplace and unbridled speculation; to the gigantic mass of nonrecyclable human detritus that would soon be exported in shipping containers to the Third World to save the ecosystem of the First and put a stop to its environmental degradation; to those condemned to live in shacks next to dump heaps of toxic waste because they themselves were highly toxic dross and dregs; to the excreta of the social body who, after being compressed and ground to bits in the stomach and intestines of the powerful, fell down the precipice of the rectum into the latrines.

Yes, we are turds, fecal matter, the sight and odor of which offend the eyes and noses of the beautiful people! Contaminated and irradiated by their laboratories and industries, we cannot even be used as manure to fertilize their fields! They should bury us underneath solid cement blocks so that we don't corrupt their water, their earth, and their air, unless those gentlemen who solicit our votes in order to get to the top of the ladder resort to the fourth and most efficacious of the elements: fire! Reducing us to ashes in enormous incinerators!

The horde of beggars had now invaded the street, traffic had been blocked at the Rue du Château d'Eau, and our wretched hero was delighted to catch the grim look that the statue of Saint Anthony, with his little pig and crook, was casting in the direction of the Defecator's splendid speaker's stand.

We represent the International of excreta, the stinking turds of the new planetary order! We are fragmented, dispersed, they can sweep us away with their water hoses and then sterilize the ground with disinfectants and pesticides! If we are united, they won't be able to flush us down the drain!

(The roar of the crowd drowned out the howl of distant police sirens. Were there massed riot squads in the Gare de l'Est as certain excited rumormongers claimed?)

Listen to me, all of you! Our foul-smelling tide will invade your streets, will advance as irresistibly as the lava of volcanoes, will paralyze the flow of your traffic, will immobilize your beautifully tailored executives on the sidewalks, will surround the sacred temple of the stock market and silence the cries of its worshipers, will fill your mansions with a stench that will chase the inhabitants out and then infiltrate the offices of banks till it reaches the safe deposit boxes and transmutes the gold and the banknotes into shit!

Was it the violence of the applause with which the beggars in rags greeted these words or the inopportune ringing of the doorbell by the gas man or by the accursed woman who lived next door that woke him? He poked his head out of the sheets as cautiously as a turtle and his roving gaze wandered around the room until it landed on the luminous numbers on the dial of the alarm clock.

It was 8 A.M. on the dot.

A persistent doubt tormented him: demagogue or prophet? When you came right down to it, who was the Defecator?

Second Dream

You climb the stairway of the employment agency with your briefcase full of documents, diplomas and university degrees, work certificates and good conduct reports, a résumé as solid as the carapace of a crustacean. On the steps leading to the lower landings an incalculable number of insubstantial shades, jobless souls, emaciated, toughened by patience, kneaded down by resignation, are crowded together, one on top of the other. Before coming they have brushed their tattered suits and shoes with gaping soles, smoothed with their fingers or a near-toothless comb their hirsute tangle of hair, refreshed in the basin of a public fountain their purulent faces lined with a network of broken blood vessels. They hide the telltale signs of their poverty with patches and bits of string, accept their precarious situation with humble and silent dignity.

You glimpse among them an old acquaintance: the elderly gentleman camped out on the boulevard. He has ironed his threadbare suit worn to the warp from use and is wearing an outlandish hat, no doubt rescued from one of the trash cans near the workshops of the garment manufacturers. He has also gathered together letters and printed matter and tied a ribbon around them: proof of jobs held long ago, certificates of residence years out of date, old photographs of himself, dim and yellowed. He has seated himself on the top step, just below the landing, but younger, more battle-hardened postulants brutally keep him from moving any higher.

Next you see middle-aged men and women, carefully dressed, the possessors of more believable credentials. The contretemps of being unemployed, they claim, is a happenstance, a matter of sheer chance, like a cold caught out of imprudence and easily medicated. In order to rid themselves of any and every sign of chronic and perhaps incurable illness, they have paid careful attention to their attire and perfected their smile, with the professionalism of models applying for an assignment at an advertising agency. They want to inspire confidence, to radiate optimism, convince the employees of the employment agency of their faith in the system and the brilliance of their prospects once they've recovered from the absurd misstep that sent them sprawling.

Still higher up, in an anxious semicircle around the door leading into the office of the agency, a crowd of executives with expensive briefcases, gray suits, ties, shirts with starched collars, rehearse their presentation number, their gifts of persuasion, the orderly exposition of their merits, work experience, abilities. Those who have a smattering of English or speak the language well show off their dazzling expertise in the areas of marketing and the competitive arts. But the fog that gradually invades the stairway blurs them; their aptitudes and talents pale, become tenuous and frangible, vanish into thin air as in a mirage.

You make your way amid their insubstantial silhouettes and enter the office. Here everything is modern, aseptic, and functional. Uniformed hostesses that put you in mind of flight attendants glide among the visitors on roller skates; their bell skirts remind you of ballerinas' tutus adorned with ostrich feathers. One of them, quick and efficient, takes charge of you: she guides you down a long corridor lined with mirrors and abruptly comes to a stop with a pirouette, resting her weight on the white tip of her ankle boot.

In the office into which she ushers you, a young man, dressed in a white smock and wearing glasses in a gold frame, awaits you, seated on the other side of a desk whose surface is covered with telephones, fax machines, and computers. With a friendly gesture, he invites you to sit in the armchair reserved for job seekers.

He (with a fixed smile): I'm listening, I'm all ears.

You (self-assured): I've brought my curriculum vitae and documents supporting it. As you will see, I am a graduate of the University of . . .

He (curt): leave all that on the desk! Your degrees are of no interest to me. What is your astrological sign?

You (confused): I believe I'm a Capricorn.

He (stern): do you merely believe so or is it a verifiable fact?

You (determined to show your self-confidence): I shall prove it to you immediately if you will permit me to.

He (holding your documentation in his hand): those born under this sign are reputed to be stubborn, secretive, and taciturn. Do you recognize these characteristics in yourself?

You (dubious): well, in all truth . . .

He (suave): on what day and at what hour were you born?

You (reeling the information off): on the fifth day of January at 10:30 P.M.!

He (once again stern): I am going to put these data in my computer. Meanwhile, go on into the next room. My assistant will give you a series of tests.

You obey his instructions and wait in a little room furnished only with a desk and two chairs; the absence of temperature charts, X rays, and medical equipment worries you. What sort of tests do they intend to subject you to? The arrival of another skater with an ostrich-plume tail banishes your misgivings. She has in her hands a record containing pages with handwriting on them and others that are blank and places them on the desk.

She: you're about to take the handwriting test. Listen to me carefully: copy the pages with handwriting on them onto the blank ones, taking care not to skip so much as a comma. When you've finished, press the call button. Once the manager has a sample of your handwriting and your astrological chart in hand, he will decide.

You sit down at the desk and take a look at the contents of the record: the manuscript pages are in your own hand and you note the title with a start: "Prolegomena to an apocalypse"!

This discovery bewilders you: why copy what you yourself have already written? Overcoming your fears and doubts you summon the hostess.

You: señorita, I am the author of these pages!

She: prove it! Copy half a dozen lines before my eyes!

You obey with resignation: what does all this have to do with the position you are applying for?

You (interrupting your transcription): I'm not going to bore myself or bore readers with a text they've already read. In my opinion this little sample is more than sufficient.

She: Okay. I'll take it to the manager this minute. Meanwhile, relax, do some yoga! He'll summon you in a few minutes.

You: do I have any hopes of getting a job?

She: What in the world are you talking about? We're not here to find a job for anybody. Our work is in the field of synesthesia, bilocalization, multiple personalities, and astrology! Every human being is born at precisely the same time as his virtual enemy. We determine who that person is, where he or she was born, where he or she lives, what his or her profession and sex are, so as to put the two of them in touch with each other!

You: all that is absurd!

She: not at all! Each of them is unaware of the existence of the other, unless they are twins or the sheerest of chances has brought them together. An infinitesimal possibility, as you can imagine. Your astrological chart and sample handwriting are a great help to us. I caution you that we cannot guarantee with absolute certainty that the two of you will meet. But if we succeed in bringing this meeting about, the shock will be unavoidable. No human being is able to escape this reciprocal gravitation!

The hostess does a half-pirouette on her skates and disappears amid a whirl of feathers and a rustle of silk, leaving you all alone in the phantasmal room.

Report by the Major (III)

As soon as dawn broke—after going without sleep all night long, absorbed in reading the manuscripts found in the suitcase—I presented myself, accompanied by my British colleague M. R., at what had once been the main post office building, at present situated at the front line of the besieged city. It was a splendid day, and through the peephole of our armored personnel carrier I could make out the spiteful skeletons of the burned-out buildings, the rusted carcasses of vehicles and streetcars reduced to scrap metal by scorching flames. The blinding white snow that was falling seemed to dissolve in the transparent air. The city's inhabitants remained huddled in their houses and along the entire avenue I saw only half a dozen feeble, miserably ill silhouettes. Every so often the rattle of machine gun fire broke the fragile silence with its earsplitting clatter.

After a brief exchange with the officers and cadres whom we were relieving, we crossed no-man's-land, the geography of desolation: streetcar tracks leading nowhere; twisted, half-coiled cables; gap-toothed, disfigured, or one-eyed houses; leafless trees that no one is even bothering to cut down. The Egyptian and Jordanian contingent in the personnel carrier remained as silent and withdrawn as I was.

At his field office protected by sandbags, the colonel gave us the day's briefing: no incident had been reported since the evening before and the scheduled flights had taken off and landed with no problems. I went to my office and carefully scrutinized all of the passenger lists of recent weeks. The three Spaniards whose names appear on them are two known journalists and a member of Doctors Without Borders whose heated and unthinking opinions regarding the role of the International Mediation Force in the conflict I openly opposed a few days ago during a dinner. If the dead and vanished "J. G." arrived in the city, he had to have gone overland, carrying false papers, in the one convoy bringing humanitarian aid that the besiegers permitted to pass through the lines several months ago.

The obscurity in which this affair is shrouded continues to grow and each day brings new evidence that belies our previous conjectures. The few proofs we have at hand are scarcely reliable: the English translation, for instance, of the death certificate that I took it upon myself to order, left me completely perplexed. How is it possible that the medical examiner drew up the certificate and signed it without specifying the exact cause of death? Why did he describe the dead man's identity as "unknown" instead of asking for his passport to be sent up from the reception desk? Why didn't the receptionist notice its disappearance before I arrived on the scene?

As I was busy taking care of the day's routine business—sending a delegation of officers to the barracks of the besiegers to discuss security at the airport—the idea occurred to me to have a look at the bag full of mail that has been confiscated in the last few days. By virtue of a confidential decision made by the high command, those journalists and members of the ONG, the nongovernmental organization, who were in the habit of leaving S. with packets of letters deposited at the reception desk of the H. I. by the inhabitants of this city cut off from the outside world, are now permitted to take only six of them with them; if they have more than that number, they are confiscated from them at the airport and gather dust in a mail sack in the office next to the one I use when I am on duty.

Without any great conviction, but with a certain secret hope, I began to examine the letters one by one—there were hundreds, of all shapes and sizes, addressed to spouses, parents, children, brothers and sisters, relatives or friends of those besieged—until I came across one envelope, the mere sight of which gave me a start: the one addressed to a certain "J. G.," Boîte Postale 435, PTT, Boulevard de Bonne Nouvelle, 75010 Paris. Although the sender's name and address were written in Arabic characters, the addressee's name and address were in handwriting identical to that of the annotations of the manu-script found in the suitcase! With an excitement that is readily understandable, I laid it on the desk with trembling hand. It was an ordinary envelope, beige, coarse-textured, of average size, containing a number of typewritten pages weighing approximately 100 grams. I locked the door of my office from the inside: I had a presentiment of the importance of this discovery and did not wish to be interrupted as I read through these pages. A brief glance at the contents convinced me that the owner of the suitcase and the author of the missive were one and the same person. But my bewilderment reached its height when I realized that the text being sent to "J. G." corresponded word for word to the contents of the first pages of the present book.

District Under Siege

He was awakened by the muffled echo of gunfire. He stretched his arm out and pressed the button on the lamp, but the bulb didn't light up. Still half asleep, he fumbled about for his slippers, and drew the curtain aside before opening the blinds. It was just getting light, and the silence of the deserted street surprised him: not a pedestrian or a car in sight, despite the fact that it was the hour when the shops opened. Leaning his head out the window to the left, he discovered that traffic on the boulevard had been blocked off. Barbed wire and *chevaux-de-frise* had been placed between the side wall of the movie theater and the half-destroyed café on the corner. The front line appeared to be located there. He could not continue his investigation because the whistle of a bullet passing by that missed his head by just a few centimeters forced him to step back. As he hastily closed the window he heard the bullet hit the wall of the building next door and ricochet off it. Who, and why, had someone chosen him as a target?

He dressed in the semidarkness after checking that the power cut extended over a wide area. The elevator remained abnormally quiet; in the buildings opposite, occupied by immigrants, he could not see a single light. Fortunately, the gas was still on and he was able to make himself a cup of coffee. Thanks to his foresight or his intuition, his larder was chock full of emergency supplies. At least I'm not going to go hungry, he told himself selfishly.

Someone was rapping on the door. His next-door neighbor, disheveled and in her bathrobe, was the living image of terror. The district was under siege, she sobbed. During the night they had erected barricades on the boulevards and snipers posted in neighboring districts were shooting at anything that moved. She had seen a poor gentleman who had come outdoors to walk his dog fall to the ground, and the *esniper*—that was how she pronounced the word, her voice trembling—had finished his job by shooting the doggie to stop his whimpering. Imagine being that cruel to an innocent little creature! The situation was the same all over the district; she had just phoned to a friend on the Boulevard Sébastopol and there too there were victims, hidden snipers, and electrified barbed wire! He poured the water, still boiling hot, into a second cup and plunged a bag of lime flower tea into it. The neighbor lady—a retired civil service worker who had been widowed years before and often hinted between sighs that his status as a confirmed bachelor could easily be remedied—appeared to be about to collapse. She had naively thought that such horrors existed only on TV, in exotic cities accustomed to such things, but right down there on the street outside what was going on was really incredible. Two hundred thousand people trapped like guinea pigs in the middle of the capital of the country! The radio had merely broadcast a brief communiqué, inserted among the other news items of the day and the usual commercials, without explaining or commenting on the causes of the violence. It was obvious that orders were coming from very high up: on the morning talk show, where they always discussed everything under the sun, no one had even mentioned the siege. They want to play the whole thing down, drown it in a tidal wave of ordinary news!: the floods in Italy, the world tennis championship, the spectacular rise of the stock market thanks to the government's policy of austerity and its bold cuts in social programs.

Nobody seems to give a damn about the siege and bombardment of our district! If all this were happening in the Balkans or the Arab world, I'd understand perfectly, but, answer me this, my friend, how can they tolerate such atrocities in our own country!

He did his best to calm her and saw her to her apartment next door; though she was still racked with sobs, contrary to what he feared she did not take advantage of the opportunity to faint in his arms. He needed a little peace and quiet to think things over and make plans, but the excited conversations on the landing and visits from other neighbors prevented his doing so. All of them contributed new information about the strange situation they were experiencing: dozens of corpses were piled up on the Boulevard de Bonne Nouvelle; an entire family on Sentier had been wiped out by a mortar shell; snipers posted on the roof of the post office were methodically finishing off the wounded; the Red Cross ambulances couldn't get past the front line; the official spokesmen minimized what was happening and reiterated the authorities' determination to defend republican order. This is only the beginning, the former police officer on the second floor said, as though hinting that he was privy to secret information and knew what was going on behind the scenes. This siege may last for months and months!

Worn out by this pointless babble, the tenants in the building went back to their apartments. What else could they do except await the unpredictable course of events? The son of the bald gentleman who sold insurance policies had crossed the Rue de la Lune at lightning speed and raced under cover of the dilapidated buildings to the nearest police station. From the seemingly empty windows of the façades, dozens of pairs of eyes followed his trajectory and saw him return a few minutes later, still as fast on his feet as before, but with a look of vast annoyance on his face. The police theoretically responsible for protecting them had deserted their posts after disconnecting the phone lines and destroying their electronic database! It was all a plot cooked up by shady real estate agents and old pols; the siege had been carefully programmed!

The stupefaction of the residents of the district proved stronger than their weeping and wailing. Such an atrocity in the homeland of human rights left them dumbfounded. The representatives of neighborhood associations sent to negotiate with the enemy didn't even get as far as the barricades. Loudspeakers set up on the other side of the boulevard ordered them to clear the battlefield immediately or be swept away by mortar fire. Another wave of impromptu mediators with pacifist convictions was captured or mowed down by snipers. The number of victims grew by the day. For lack of cemeteries and in view of the refusal of the besiegers to bury the corpses it was necessary to dig common graves in vacant lots and filthy little public squares. You know I'm not a racist, the neighbor lady kept repeating like a recording, but the idea of resting for all eternity alongside a Turk or a black turns my stomach! If we can't even be buried decently, it might have been better for us never to have been born, I tell myself. We've suffered too much in this life to be buried in one big heap along with people of different races and customs!

He listened to her impassively, giving no signs either of agreement or disagreement, hoping against hope that she wouldn't bring up yet again the subject of their supposed communion of souls—a prelude to the much more threatening and concrete subject of the communion of their bodies—or fall into one of her usual fainting spells, an ideal pretext not to budge from his apartment. Our character was all ears: the lightning-swift siege of the district aroused his energy and imagination. A strange feeling of happiness had come over him and he did his best to hide it. The situation was, to be sure, no laughing matter. The dispensaries and clinics, according to the nurse on the sixth floor, were jam-packed: serums, coagulants, and anesthetics were becoming scarce. Operations were being performed in daylight, in front of the windows, at the risk of the operating room being hit by a shell or of someone in it moving into the line of sight of a sniper. The wounded were lying on stretchers, crowded together like animals in the corridors and on the stairways.

There were also food shortages: the supermarkets and warehouses located in less dangerous areas had been besieged by housewives and speculators of all sorts, quick to fish in troubled waters and make a bundle at the expense of others. They appear to be Jews, the neighbor lady had said; not all of them, of course, because I personally am acquainted with several who are good-hearted, as decent as you and I are, but anybody can see that they're a minority!

Improvised defense committees made every effort to impose a semblance of order in the chaos caused by the speculation and anarchy. Bread and other basic foodstuffs were rationed: each household had to record the quantities received in a little book stamped with an official seal. Half a dozen counterfeiters of official rubber stamps ended up getting caught and put in the public jails, that is to say in the basements of bombed buildings. According to the rumors whispered from neighbor to neighbor they were Pakistanis or Kurds.

The shortages and privations grew worse when it turned cold. In middle-class buildings like his, there was no longer any heating because of lack of fuel and the tenants bundled themselves up in blankets or warmed their numbed hands over little alcohol burners and gas rings. They're used to the cold temperatures of their countries, the attorney's wife said, pointing bitterly at the unhealthful buildings used as sweatshops and at the attics and tiny rooms where large families of immigrants from Anatolia lived crowded together, but we haven't seen anything like this since the Occupation. To stay warm they burn anything, cardboard packing boxes, newspapers, books, and I don't know what-all! One of these days they're going to cause a fire that could easily spread to this side of the street, and who's going to put it out if the besiegers won't even allow firemen through?

The possibility of calling family members and friends in other districts—the neighbor lady's eternal litany of moans and groans as she sat glued to her elegant white telephone all day long—was a double-edged sword. It allowed people to describe how incredible and horrible the situation was—with the hope, soon thwarted, of provoking *extramuros*, acts of protest and solidarity—but over time it was even more discouraging to the besieged to tumble to the fact that their drama and hardships moved no one. News of the siege had gradually disappeared from the daily news programs on television and the ones that the lucky owners of a battery radio could tune in on; once in a while when the carnage had been particularly horrendous, a brief mention of it surfaced, as if it were a minor incident of no more than passing interest. Tragedies that go on for too long are boring, a wholesaler whose shop had been destroyed by a shell remarked resignedly. The novelty of the day cancels out the one of the night before and public opinion couldn't care less that we're being hunted down like rabbits!

The facts appeared to prove him right. The tenants of his building had discovered, at first with astonishment and later with indignation, that the life of the city continued to follow its normal course. On the radio commentators spoke of the new movies just out, of concerts and recitals and sports events! More shocking still: the subway lines that crossed or bordered the district ran regularly. The only stations that had been closed were the ones located in the district itself or on the periphery of it: Montmartre, Bonne Nouvelle, Strasbourg–Saint Denis, Sentier, Réaumur-Sébastopol. A simple handwritten notice informed subway users that they were closed, without specifying the reasons why. They're treating us as though we had the plague, the nurse said indignantly. How can it be that no one is intervening or moving so much as a finger to help us? We aren't in Cambodia or Rwanda after all!

The day when they cut off the gas and the telephone, the morale of the tenants of the building, already shaky now that the siege had gone on for nine months, plummeted. Our character had foreseen this turn of events and piled on yet more pants and pullovers over the ones he already wore till he had more layers than an onion. Alone in his apartment, he went over the vicissitudes of the day in his mind and then went out to the filthy stairway littered with broken glass to hear his neighbors' comments. Had the hidden hand that guided the siege and stifled the voice of its victims resolved to increase its pressure on the district by cutting it off completely? It was all a matter of conjectures. The one certain fact was that the telephone lines had been cut and a hail of projectiles fell shortly thereafter on the commercial artery of the district. After that warning—which the media, with suspicious unanimity, failed to report so as not to alarm, it was rumored, investors and tourists—the owners of the once prosperous and well-stocked butcher shops and grocery stores crowded with customers that lined the Rue de Montorgueil lowered, permanently this time, their metal shutters.

Barricaded in their homes, the residents of the district pondered, with growing anxiety and feelings of guilt, the possible causes of the punishment that had befallen them. What crime had they committed to be subjected to such a barbarous siege? Why were they being treated like Africans without papers, Islamists, AIDS sufferers, or junkies? They hate us because we're prosperous and live in peace with immigrants! the hairdresser on three, married for twenty years to an Arab, said. At the downstairs door of the building lay the bullet-riddled corpse of another North African and no ambulance corps came to pick it up and bury it. It's all their fault! the neighbor lady from next door decreed, struggling to contain her tears with her handkerchief. If they'd stayed in their own countries instead of coming to ours, we wouldn't be suffering as we are today! You, my friend, know my thoughts on the subject: I've never been a racist, but facts are facts. Who gave this neighborhood a bad reputation? The foreigners here! Who attacked my sister-in-law, may she rest in peace, with a knife the last time she came to see me? An Arab! Who tried to rape the widow on eight in the elevator? An African! Who sells drugs and shoots up on the Rue de Saint Denis and in the corridors of the metro? Immigrants! They're the ones who've brought us disgrace and now we innocents are paying for their sins! They're the ones responsible for the siege!

(He listened to her as a person listens to rain falling and mentally noted her most flowery phrases in order to write them down later in his memo book.)

The silence that enveloped everything having to do with the siege began to be more painful than the siege itself. Neither the government nor the mayor of the capital nor the deputy to the National Assembly elected to represent the district voiced any condemnation whatever: the debates on the state of the nation, in which the spokesmen of the opposition did not refrain from offering the harshest criticisms of the party in power, made no mention of the subject. The independent radio stations, the reporters whose specialty was burning issues of the day, and even the inhabitants of neighboring districts took part in the plot: the son of the insurance agent somehow came by a new supply of batteries and invited the neighbors in to eyeball his TV set. Horse races, results of the parimutuel, semifinals of the soccer matches for the Europe Cup, the runway of the latest fashion show, the award ceremony for the Oscars, an American serial whose plot line was centered on the Miami mafia, animated cartoons, game shows, *Sesame Street*, roundtables, reality shows: the siege of the Second Arrondissement had been dropped altogether. According to the blonde on six, the former mistress of a high official at UNESCO, the Committee of Public Safety of the district had sent the secretary general of the United Nations and the president of the International Tribunal at the Hague a detailed report on the war crimes and the staggering number of violations of human rights that had taken place in the arrondissement without receiving any reply. They have nothing but contempt for us and put us in the same class as Sarajevo or Chechnya, the nurse remarked in exasperation. Our situation doesn't affect their vital interests and as a result they don't lift a finger!

The arrival of spring brought renewed mortar attacks and redoubled the fury of the snipers, but it also fed the widespread hope for a truce, for the beginning of possible peace talks. The problem lay in the fact that no one knew what the demands of the aggressors were. The aggression had been staged without any explicit motive: it therefore fell to those aggressed against to discover the reasons why they were under siege. For lack of concrete proofs and solid arguments, the hypotheses and suspicions came to focus on the heterogeneous—the former police-man called it cosmopolitan—composition of the district. Should immigrants and foreigners be cleared out of the district altogether so as to facilitate the demolition of its decrepit build-ings rented out for miserable sums, and thus make it easier for voracious speculators and real estate holding companies to make fat profits by remodeling them? Many people thought so and spoke loudly of the need for ethnic cleansing brigades. The foreigners residing in his building no longer dared to take the stairs for fear of provoking the wrath of their neighbors and finding themselves accused of being the cause of every last one of their trials and tribulations.

Since our friends can't summon up the courage to take the district by assault and do the dirty work, we'll do it ourselves! the ex-policeman said. He had gotten together with other former colleagues and sympathizers in the neighborhood and they had begun to draw up a detailed list of allogeneic buildings and of foreigners who had sneaked into buildings with pre-dominantly native tenants. Our puny hero was invited to one of the meetings and went to it with the pocket recorder he some-times used to record the monologues of the lady who lived next door before transcribing them into his memo book. We must proceed methodically, promptly, and efficiently, the former po-liceman explained to his disciples. To begin with, we'll draw up a list of buildings inhabited exclusively by immigrants and send it to the besiegers, with all the buildings pinpointed on a map so that they can blow them to pieces with their mortars. The maps must be 100 percent accurate so that they can hit their target without risking the lives of innocent victims or causing collat-eral damage. After that we'll take care of the foreigners who have infiltrated buildings with a majority of tenants who are native citizens.

There are many Jews and Armenians who have been natural-ized for generations, the nurse said. Wouldn't it be unfair to lump them together with the immigrants who are aliens?

From now on it is the *jus sanguinis* that will apply! the ex-policeman curtly interrupted her. There will be no naturalization documents worth the paper they're written on! A thick-lipped nigger with all his papers in order will still be a thick-lipped nigger. Do I make myself clear or don't I?

Everything was perfectly clear: a few timid voices raised in protest were immediately silenced. The decisions were going to be voted on by a show of hands, that is to say, approved unanimously. In a first phase, those apartments harboring allogeneic and newly arrived immigrants would be marked with a distinctive sign and those living in them would have their precious ration card taken away from them.

What about their wives and children? asked the son of the insurance agent, whose live-in girlfriend was the fruit of a mixed marriage.

There will be no exception whatsoever. It'll be a clean sweep!

The old print shop on the Rue de la Lune, located in a basement, had not been hit by mortar shells, and the district ethnic cleansing brigade ordered from it various models of placards adorned with a crescent moon, the star of David, or an African totem that would serve to indicate the origin of the foreigners. The case of Christian Armenians and Buddhist Hindus raised a number of doubts.

We will simply indicate that they're aliens without going into details! the erstwhile policeman declared. The important thing is to have them on record.

After the meeting the neighbor lady came to our petty hero's apartment. The besiegers were bearing down relentlessly on the buildings near the Porte Saint Denis and the muffled chatter of machine guns could be heard. Why not mount an assault once and for all and eliminate those who must be eliminated! Many people from here want to help them and collaborate with them. God forbid that you take me for an extremist, a proponent of violence! But the use of force in moderation is sometimes the lesser evil, don't you agree?

(Yes, despite the food shortages and her chronic ailments, the neighbor lady had not lost weight—her legs, as solid as pillars, still firmly supported her. And her complaints came thicker and faster than ever.)

It's been a year, do you realize that? We've been caught in this rattrap for a year, without being able to walk along the boulevards or go shopping at La Samaritaine or get a breath of fresh air on the Champs Elysées! As a matter of fact, I dreamed just last night that you invited me to have dinner at a brasserie in Montparnasse with musicians in tuxedos, a distinguished clientele, elegant waiters!

And what was on the menu? our hero asked suavely.

She ignored the interruption: When I woke up and saw my apartment, that luxurious candy box that my poor husband, may he rest in peace, decorated, without heat or electricity now, dreary, covered with dust, I almost exploded! If he had been a man of an age to take up arms, I think he would have gone out onto the balcony with a rifle and fired on those pigsties across the street, on that Turkish couple who keep constantly copulating and making babies! I, who have never been a racist, cannot bear them another minute, jammed together in their miserable apartment like a litter of guinea pigs! They and the other immigrants who use and abuse our hospitality to procreate and fill our maternity clinics and hospitals to overflowing have ruined the country and provoked the just reaction of its patriots, of the forces that are laying siege to us out of fear that we will contaminate them!

The identification of foreigners and immigrants took place without incident. The ex-policeman supervised the proper execution of the orders with his old regulation army revolver and organized tenant patrols that went up and down the stairs at regular intervals. This is worse than the Occupation, one pensioner of Jewish origin murmured when she discovered the six-pointed star defacing the door of her apartment. What do they intend to do next: begin staging raids again?

Everyone was waiting for the agressors' answer: the implacable bombing of the buildings marked as targets. Some of the tenants of the building kept watch on them with binoculars and ran to the half-open window every time they heard the whistle of a bullet or the deafening explosion of a mortar or artillery shell. They're setting up the operation in a well-calculated and scientific way, the former policeman reassured everyone. When they begin the all-out attack, there'll be no fooling around: they won't leave one of them alive! And then our time will have come: every last rat will be flushed out of its hole!

But help from outside—the liberating intervention of the aggressors—was a long time coming: the siege went on for yet another year and the snipers continued to choose their targets at will. An entire native family perished when their apartment was hit by heavy-caliber cannon fire. On the other hand, their Arab neighbors had not suffered the slightest damage. It was obviously an error, a tragic error! but how to raise the morale of the residents of the district if the shortage of everything grew worse and another winter was coming on? The ethnic cleansing brigades advocated beginning their job without waiting for the all-out attack; however, the shortage of arms and their own state of physical weakness—only two bakeries were making bread and the price of food on the black market was sky-high—convinced them of the uselessness of their plan. All they could do was wait.

One morning, at the time of day when housewives were in the habit of heating their family's meager rations of canned corned beef, a gift from the European Community, the building trembled as if from an earthquake. The last windowpanes left undamaged after two years of siege shattered into a thousand pieces. Lamps, pictures, shelves, and even heavy standing wardrobes crashed to the floor. Our character clung heroically to his bed, added another blanket to the ones he already had over him, and lay there as if bundled up in a cocoon.

A shell had exploded in the gigantic movie theater—closed since the beginning of the siege—on the corner adjacent to the building, causing its glowing emblematic tower, the pride of the district, to collapse. That attack, with no military objective whatsoever, stupefied them. The movie theater was located right on the boulevard, on the front line: therefore its destruction could not be attributed to erroneous targeting. It had been aimed, consciously and deliberately, in order to deprive the district of what had been its symbol: a real act of memoricide! Minutes later, mortars and grenade launchers finished the work of demolition: the neon signs and the faded old posters advertising Walt Disney and Vanessa Paradis came tumbling down. The neighbor lady knocked at the door of his study, her chest heaving with sobs. Unable to bear her laments, our melancholy hero silently drew the bolt shut and waited, holding his breath, to hear the rustle of her bathrobe as she headed back to her fancy candy box.

The managing committee of the building summoned its crisis unit: although he was not invited to the meeting, our protagonist slipped in with his pocket recorder at the ready. The tenants who were natives of the district needed a plausible explanation, followed by precise directives, if their faith was to remain intact. But the former policeman, usually extroverted and authoritarian, didn't even open his mouth. They had to bow to the evidence: his calculations had turned out to be as erroneous as his emergency measures were useless. The signals of connivance sent to the besiegers in the hope of making peace with them had not had the slightest effect. The questions from his bewildered and alarmed supporters were left unanswered. The former policeman stared into space with clouded eyes: according to a number of those who had attended the meeting, his breath reeked of cheap brandy.

It was the beginning of the end. Having lost their leader, the purifiers did not know what to do or what saint to pray to. Scowling, the neighbor lady finally pointed to other factors that were to blame: syringes, condoms, H.I.V. positives, promiscuous homosexuals and heterosexuals. The siege was punishment from heaven. People had strayed from the path of righteousness, their amorality and dissipation cried out for vengeance: numerous couples were living in a state of sin, without benefit of clergy!; girls dressed and behaved like stumpets—strumpets, our protagonist gently corrected her—; young men took drugs and attended pornographic shows!; a person couldn't go out on the street without stumbling over indecent inverts! A member of the Evangelical Mission "Healing and Salvation" strongly supported her : yes, the lady is right! What is happening to us is a manifestation of divine wrath, like the fire that destroyed the two accursed cities of the plains! The individual fell on his knees to pray for mercy, gradually imitated by the tenants gathered on the half-ruined stairway. Making a painful effort, the neighbor lady had also knelt and was reciting the Pater Noster and the Credo. Because of the shards of glass strewn all over, a number of the penitents were bleeding. A priest, summon a priest! the attorney's wife, overcome with hysteria, cried. An elderly woman went in search of a reliquary and a flagon of holy water from Lourdes. The price of little sacred prints with prayers and indulgences below them rapidly mounted. The tenants of the building lined up in the apartment of the man selling them under the counter and grabbed them out of each others' hands. The singing of psalms, the reciting of litanies, and the beating of breasts went on all night long.

The shell had also rent the harmony of certain families: the hairdresser on three who was married to an Arab heaped insults on him and ordered him out of their apartment. The children of a mixed marriage wept in despair: their schoolmates refused to say hello to them and accused them of having AIDS. At dawn, a heavy downpour coming in through French doors and windows forced the frenzied worshipers and penitents to break off their prayers: their apartments risked being flooded.

The siege would soon have lasted a thousand and one days and there was no Sheherazade to tell the story of it. Our character was writing his own but he was unable to find an ending for it. He spent several days mulling the problem over till finally he received unexpected help. Someone had managed to procure the latest issue of the *Entertainment Guide* with a detailed listing of theaters, cinemas, concert halls, museums, exhibitions of the plastic arts, monuments, boat rides on the Seine, famous restaurants, and cabarets. Each district was accorded the honor of a special column that listed, marked with one, two, or three asterisks, depending on their interest and importance, the places worth visiting and a history and succinct description of each. The column describing his district, marked with a little square indicating that a visit to it was not worthwhile, contrasted with the others by virtue of its brevity. It read:

DISTRICT UNDER SIEGE

Third Dream

You roam the district from one end to the other, in the grip of a feeling of helplessness and torment, aware that its ruin is imminent, that its irremediable devastation is approaching, its fury held in check. How to convince your fellow citizens that catastrophe is close at hand if no one listens now to prophets dressed in rags, despite their bold eloquence, their exemplary fervor? You are looking for the place where madness can wander freely until it reaches the confines of wisdom and sanctity. An affluent society detests your eccentricities, scorn for appearances, proudly exalted sodomy, public exhibition of vices, offensive desire for sincerity.

How to shake it from its lethargy and make it understand that you belong to the secret community whose virtue keeps the world from collapsing and whose teachings open up the path to goodness and tolerance? Must you imitate Chiblí and set fire to the tail of a donkey to indicate that everything is the handiwork of God and therefore worthy of respect and admiration? Recite the maxims of Sidi Slimâne al-Jazûli, with their mordant praise of the temperance and probity of the canine species? Climb up onto a fairgrounds stand and play the clown or the teller of tales, like that Muslim judge from Seville who abandoned possessions, family, and country to live amid poor and innocent children?

What does it matter if, owing to your strident provocation, harsh imprecations, conduct alien to all human respect, they call you sorcerer, charlatan, impostor! You drink cheap brandy, you breathe the fumes of a rag soaked in ether, you afford people glimpses of your behind and skinny legs through rips and tears that, despite their resemblance to those shown in ads for a popular brand of jeans, lack their touch of refinement and adolescent chic? Like a fakir or a wandering dervish, you wear your shoe soles out tramping along the boulevards, you shock the pharisees with your incongruities, you point your bony, accusing index finger at their lives of smug self-satisfaction. Are you a pitiful epileptic, as was said of Sidi Abderrahman al-Majdoub or like him have you reached the ultimate experience, the stammering of one thunderstruck by the certainty of his mission?

Little by little, a nucleus of initiates surrounds you, follows your hallucinated footsteps, galvanizes and gathers new disciples. The black leaning against the statue of Saint Anthony has recovered from the effects of his overdose, and with his baseball cap, is walking on the arm of the plain, angular girl who rolled him so skillfully. Other drug addicts, their syringes still stuck into their veins, file along after them in silent meditation. The fragile, almost brittle silhouettes of AIDS victims seem transparent, subtle bodies. Illegal immigrants, men without jobs, indigents without a fixed abode, join the cortege en masse with placards and slogans of protest. Those crippled and disabled by secret experiments of the military-industrial complex denounce technoscientific fundamentalism. Fugitives from ethnic purification sum up the horrors of the tragedy in a Bosnian flag soaked in blood. Right-thinking citizens flee this sector of the city or fearfully barricade themselves inside their homes.

The demonstrators now occupy the entire boulevard. But even though the city is quiet, crouched over in fear, it is not yours: police sirens wail deafeningly; riot squads, equipped with helmets and shields, cut you off on the right, on the left, in front and behind; tear gas is commingled with toxic clouds that affect the respiratory system and cause blindness. Where to go if helicopters roar to the point of paroxysm inside your own head?; go down into the metro, infiltrate the entrails of the monster, lose yourselves in the twists and turns of its intestinal labyrinth! The jobless, the beggars, the sick, the junkies take to its stairs, invade its platforms, transfer points, corridors. All of them await your directions, the hoarse voice of the old prophets. A vision illuminates you, with the inspired concision of a line of verse. You unbuckle your belt, let your pants down, expose your impressive bare ass. A raucous howl halts the molecular dispersion of the crowd gathered round you: it is the proclaimed sign.

You are, you incarnate, you embody the incandescent figure of the Defecator!

Report by the Major (IV)

The reading and rereading of the manuscripts found in the suitcase occupied the whole of my day off. I shut myself up in the room of the high command of the International Mediation Force and remained there all by myself, a stranger to everything occurring in time and space, lost in a desert of shifting dunes in which trails laboriously traced were erased by a puff of wind, leaving me without markers or points of reference in the middle of the blinding maelstrom raised by the sandstorm.

The various stories by the dead and vanished "J. G.," written in the third person though they also bore signs of the presence of an omniscient narrator, are centered around the siege, imaginary or real, of a city or a district, and have no connection whatever with the collection of poems I mentioned in my second report regarding this complicated matter.

Are all the manuscripts the work of one and the same author? I honestly couldn't answer that question. The stories and the poems express different obsessions, without any apparent common denominator. Although in the report sent to the central headquarters of the army I purposely used terminology befitting a military scale of values and principles, it does not represent, strictly speaking, my real opinion or my real sentiments concerning the poems.

In his own way, the author of the stories also expresses certain subversive points of view, not with regard to the subject of sex but to the new politicoeconomic world order and its disastrous consequences. The evocations of the Paris neighborhood in which the character lives reveal a perfect knowledge of it, an impression corroborated by the missive sent to "J. G." at a post office box the number of which, by an odd coincidence, is exactly the same as that of the room in the hotel in which death overtook him and the street address of which is that of a post office described in one of the stories. This series of coincidences and signs, instead of putting a conscientious investigator like myself on the right track, leads him astray at every turn. The narrator is not trustworthy and appears to lay a series of traps for the reader into which he inevitably falls before he realizes that he has taken the baited hook and been brought to the exact point where he was intended to be.

But it is the first text—in which the protagonist stages his death seconds before it really comes about—that turned my doubts into veritable stupefaction. How could the guest in room 435 describe his emotions and experiences during the siege and mention having set them down in writing if he was whisked away from the land of the living by the explosion of a mortar shell shortly after his arrival?

My original intention of entrusting the manuscripts to our embassy in Z. to be sent on to Spain via the diplomatic pouch was obviously impractical. The anachronisms and absurdities contained in them make the disappearance of the author an even more incredible occurrence. The reading of them would have robbed my already inconsistent reports of even their pale shadow of verisimilitude: the entire episode becomes fiction and I myself a fictitious character!

After much sober reflection, I have reached the conclusion that it will be more prudent to keep the manuscripts under lock and key and make no mention of what has happened; otherwise I risk becoming the laughingstock of the general staff. Only a possible historian-compiler, with all the scattered pieces of the puzzle in hand, would be able to put them together with the necessary patience and skill and by so doing incidentally restore my ruined credibility.

The Mortal Enemy

According to a legend that he had read as a child, every human being, at the very instant that his mother delivers him, comes into this world accompanied by his virtual enemy. This latter may be born on a different continent, be of a different race and sex, first see the light of day on the opposite side of the world. Each of them is completely unaware of the existence of the other and of the relentless hatred that binds them unless an unfortunate twist of fate brings them together. In such a case, the recognition will be instantaneous and the confrontation fatal. The secret adversary will not cease in his endeavor until he has fulfilled his destiny: wiping his counterpart and rival off the face of the earth.

At the beginning of the siege, the legend remained buried in his subconscious and rose to the surface only months later. His comfortable modern apartment in the new area of the city, immediately adjoining the front line, soon was hit by enemy artillery. The living room where he received visitors—the windows of which overlooked the river and the blocks of houses on the front line, the hideout of the snipers—was destroyed. The ensuing conflagration also badly damaged the adjoining room that he used as a dining room and left it in a precarious state, exposed to the attacks of grenade launchers and mortars. Fortunately the third room—the bedroom—was left undamaged by the brutal and violent attack. Only the pictures on the wall fell to the floor and he put them back in place after carefully sweeping the passageway that ran through the apartment from one end to the other and piling the rubble and debris in the devastated room, now opening out onto nothing but empty air.

Like his neighbors, he believed that the situation could not go on. The international community would not be able to tolerate that medieval siege with modern weapons to which, for no rational cause, they found themselves subjected. So, imitating their example, he kept cool, armed himself with patience, and began the work of cleaning up and gardening permitted him by his new status of a historian out of a job: the national library in which he did research in the archive of Arab and Ottoman manuscripts had been hit by incendiary missiles, and except for its neo-Moorish façades dating back to the Austrian era, it now was nothing but a melancholy pile of ruins.

With the aid of a hoe he had bought on the black market, he dug up soil from the gardens behind the apartment building and brought it up to the fifth floor. Bucket by bucket, he spread it out over the floor of what had been his living room, transformed it into a vegetable garden, and planted carrot seeds and onions in it. He watered them daily, carefully tending his small but comforting crop. Since the arrival of the International Mediation Force, artillery bombings and heavy arms fire were less frequent and shots rang out only sporadically, between long intervals of deceptive quiet. Only the snipers went on with their job with nothing to stop them: the troops of the multinational force whose tanks went back and forth directly below his apartment windows did nothing to silence them.

The whistle of a shell only a few centimeters above his head— when, accustomed now to exceptional circumstances that little by little had become routine, he was watering the plants of his little garden after having waited several months for the seeds to sprout—abruptly ushered in a harder and more worrisome stage of the siege. Overcome by fear, he had dropped the cooking pot he used to water his plants and sought cover by crouching down alongside the wall in the next room. Someone had shot at him from the block of buildings on the other side of the river. He grabbed his binoculars, and through the hole torn open by the explosion of the shell in the partition wall that separated the two rooms, focused one by one on the windows from which the shot had apparently come until he spied the rifle barrel with its sight aimed at his apartment. He made out a head wearing a ski mask in the shadow: the sniper had lain in wait for his chosen target with a persistence that struck fear into his heart. Why precisely him and no one else? He threw a cushion out into the passageway, in the area of the apartment within the sniper's line of sight, and the sound of the bullet as it ricocheted and buried itself in the ceiling persuaded him that his instincts had been right. The individual whose eyebrow was resting just above the sight of the rifle had chosen him as his victim. Then there surfaced from the depths of his memory the legend he had read as a child: this was no doubt his mortal enemy. The virtual threat had become a reality: now he was only 100 meters away from him. The siege of the city had brought them together.

Once the first moment of bewilderment had passed, the discovery strengthened his desire to fight back and survive. Instead of allowing himself to be overcome with despair like the majority of his neighbors after months and months of vain hopes of a hypothetical intervention from outside, the certainty of the existence of his mortal enemy on the other side of the river spurred him on. He would have to conspire against fate, thwart his enemy's plans, keep as stealthy and watchful an eye on him as the other was keeping on him.

Now that he had located the hideout that was the source of the danger, he resolved to rule his life and his movements in accord with his discovery. He spent hour after hour waiting for the rifle barrel and the masked head resting on its sight to appear; it was his program and his objective of the day, his real reason for being. The extraordinary attention on the part of the stranger of which he was the object eventually made him feel flattered. His mortal enemy was at his service day and night, scrupulously devoted all his time to him, and like the most solicitous of lovers eagerly awaited his slightest gesture.

He answered his enemy's strategy of harassment by his own strategy of a man harassed. He moved his mattress from the bedroom to the little cubbyhole next to the kitchen, where before the siege he had pored over manuscripts devoted to the life of an obscure Moroccan saint and stored his collection of books and dictionaries. He divided his time between this little room and the kitchen, busying himself heating the tasteless canned goods distributed by the various humanitarian organizations or editing fictitious versions of the siege supposedly written by an anonymous major of the International Mediation Force.

He knew that his mortal enemy was not giving up his goal. On more than one occasion, when he unexpectedly appeared in the passageway to go get something he had left in his former bedroom or to inspect the state of the dining room after the explosion of a grenade in a nearby building, the whistle of a bullet had suddenly brought him back to reality. He was obliged to remain continually on guard: any distraction could cost him his life. To spy on his enemy spying on him, he had to make a sudden dash for the former dining room and from there aim his binoculars at his hiding place. If his mortal enemy was at his post, all he could do was crouch down and wait for the silent rifle barrel to disappear from the window: his enemy too had to eat, defecate, and sleep. He could no longer go as he once had to what had been his living room to water his little garden: the sniper's rifle had a night sight, as he realized on the night when the cooking pot that he was holding was shot out of his hands by a rifle bullet that wounded him in the thumb and forced him to stretch out on the floor of the room next door until day dawned; shivering from the cold, he could see through the opening that, for just a few moments, doubtless, his enemy had left his post.

The territory he occupied in the apartment shrank like shagreen. Only the kitchen and the little study offered a vague semblance of safety. But the lack of a window in the study and the apparently permanent power outage prevented him from using it as his work space and setting himself up there. Condemned to immobility, he cooked his meals and wrote curled up in one corner of the kitchen, taking advantage of the light that came in from the rear façade of the building. The candles with which he lighted the apartment at the beginning of the siege and which allowed him the consolation of reading had become not only an impossible luxury but a fatal attraction to his enemy. His elaborate conjectures and fantasies about his double occupied his mind throughout the day. Who was he, what did he look like, had they both been shaped in the same mold? How had he sensed and incarnated the identity of an immutable enemy? Had he deciphered it by reading the stars, the lines in the palm of his hand? Or had he been enlightened, as he sometimes thought, by a sudden vision, a theatrical moment of instant recognition?

At times, he believed himself to be the victim of self-delusion: living out an experience that was the imaginary product of his schizophrenia. But the shots with which his double lying in ambush on the other side of the river regularly reminded him of his presence immediately dispelled his doubts. With a boldness bordering on irrationality, he ran along the passageway to his hiding place from which he could spy on him with the binoculars and breathed a sigh of relief: he was still there. The tiny, tenuous thread of life that united them across the front line and the river was his last and best guarantee of continuity.

Gradually cornered in a smaller and smaller area, he had limited his movements to a necessary minimum: a leap from the kitchen to the minuscule study and from there to the toilet. His swift forays into the dining room and as far as his voyeur's peephole, contrary to the most elementary caution, were his daily fix: he wouldn't have given them up for anything. He needed to make certain of the fidelity of that jealous lover, of his fervent and constant vigil. He spent days at a time keeping watch on the rifle barrel and the head covered with a ski mask. A doubt gnawed at him: did the situation of complementarity that they mutually agreed upon imply a reciprocity of feelings? Could one of the two of them subsist without the other or were their destinies as inseparable as legend had it?

Was it the intensity of this intimate debate that revealed to the sniper by telepathy how dangerous and obsessive his spying was? Or had one or another of his neighbors, a secret accomplice of those laying siege, informed on him, using a secret system of signals in code? In any event the hundred or so well-aimed rounds of rifle fire aimed at the cracks and crannies of the partition wall until it was riddled with bullet holes had achieved his purpose: to make his spying on him visible and therefore impossible. No wall now protected him from the relentlessness of his sentinel. With an overwhelming sensation of defeat, he took refuge in his miserable redoubt: the few square meters of the little cubbyhole and the inhospitable kitchen devoid of all charm.

He stayed there for several weeks, without writing, scarcely eating, his mind wholly focused on the mystery of the implacable enemy. He aged, lost weight, stopped washing himself. His face began to seem strange to him in the mirror, that hand mirror in which one morning, finally, he suddenly saw reflected in the distance the block of houses on the other side of the river, the sniper's lair, the shiny, sawed-off barrel of the rifle, the head resting as always on the sight seconds before the shot, fatal this time and final.

Report by the Major (V)

I have decided to shut myself up in my room at the residence for officers and leaders of the International Mediation Force: the violent exchanges of artillery fire in the vicinity of the Olympic stadium and the rain of shells coming from the hills on the other side of the river do not concern me. What is happening is too serious to allow me to waste precious time writing trifling reports, going on routine missions, and making inspection rounds. My insignificant presence would not alter the course of events or ameliorate the lot of this exhausted and martyrized city.

Using as an excuse a bad attack of the flu, I stayed in bed with the curtains drawn, plunged into a stimulating and fruitful darkness. I need to recover, to get my emotions and ideas in order once again. The shadow of "J. G.," of his arrival and disappearance, of the mystery that surrounds them, is a trivial concern compared to the agitation caused by an attentive rereading of his manuscripts. His depiction of the scenes of desolation left by the siege; his cruel fantasies and premonitory visions of the society that awaits us—that "New World Symphony," as he calls it with mordant irony—; the detailed description of his own death in the place where the explosion of the mortar shell took him by surprise would suffice by themselves to leave me in a state of shock and keep me from sleeping at night. But the final blow was his last story, "The Mortal Enemy": the precise reference by its main character to his task of "drafting fictitious versions of the siege supposedly written by an anonymous major of the International Mediation Force"!

How to include in the documentation to be sent to the army general staff pages that cast doubt on my reports as a whole and to top it all off turn me into a fictitious being, one who exists only on paper, a minor character mentioned by the protagonist of a story by a supposed author who has disappeared! The brutal shock of this discovery went beyond plunging me into uncertainty; it disengendered me.

During so many empty hours with no support, without a ray of light transpiercing me, I cling to the pages of the collection of poems entitled *Sotadic Zone*. I spend hours absorbed in them: the reading of them inflames me, sets me afire.

All the theophanies or images censured throughout my life at home, at school, in the army burst into the darkness of my cell with the blinding light of empowerment: the Word conjugates me.

Are these visions or precise highlights of a superior reality? Will their light last after the writing?

Sotadic Zone

In the items on the list of the major's belongings found in his almost monastic room in the residence for leaders and officers of the International Mediation Force, I found a notebook with a green cover with the typed title *Sotadic Zone.*

A quick look through it justifies the conclusion that it has been censored: one of its pages has been torn out altogether, others cut to pieces with scissors. All the verses of two poems—for the notebook in fact consists of a collection of poems—are so full of ink stains that they are illegible. In places, in the margins of the written text or in the blanks left on the pages with the ink stains, there are notes left by enraged readers or the wrathful censor: "Commie," "rotten bastard," "degenerate," "kike," "queer," and other insulting epithets and phrases. In addition, there are a variety of flowery glosses in erudite Latin, quite obviously the work of a different author.

I searched in vain among the sheets of paper thrown in the wastebasket and those piled up on the shelves of the wardrobe for expurgated pages or fragments of the text. Should I believe the major's orderly from Colombia when he assures me that he saw him swallow several pages, as did, according to legend, the author of the *Spiritual Canticle* when the Carmelites came to his cell to arrest him? In the face of the impossibility of establishing the authenticity of the facts and the origin of the mutilations undergone by the notebook—a genuine case of textual fraud—I am sending you a copy of the few verses that escaped the furious destruction, as well as the brief final poems that, for a reason unknown to me, are still intact.

During so many empty hours with no support
(without a ray of light transpiercing me)
I call to mind the lineaments of that coarse uniform, the humble
     veil of your robust attributes.

                                      (page 2)
Were they visions or precise highlights of a superior reality?

Their brightness did not last beyond the writing.

(*The Body Guard*, page 3)

The following page, suppressed altogether, had been replaced by another one, affixed to the cover of the notebook with a strip of adhesive tape: simply a Latin reproduction of the Credo, followed by a paragraph of chapter 19 of Genesis describing the destruction of the two abominable cities after the angels' visit to Lot and his family.

The pages numbered 4, 5, and 6 had a better fate. The scholiast confines himself to pointing out: *peccatum contra naturam.* Another glossarist (the handwriting is different) satirizes the declarations of Monsignor Elías Yanes concerning the lack of human dignity of homosexuals and answers Wojtylan orthodoxy with an assertion that shocked Christianity more than seven centuries ago: *Quod perfecta abstinentia ab actu carnis corrompit virtutem et speciem!*

Without prejudice to the opinion of the graphologist, I venture to state that the glossarists were three in number, unless the major had cleverly altered his own handwriting (but why?), I do not wish to lose myself in digressions, however, and reproduce below the poems that are intact:

Impossible to encompass his great chest.

> You gain access to him from the side, you make your way into
> the hirsute foliage
> Shade, undergrowth, brush.
>
> Fleece rough and untamed.
>
> Thickets easy to go astray in.
>
> Hillocks hidden in the bush.
>
> All uncultivated, left fallow.

Silviculturist

Bulbs
the stem erect, fungiform
topped with a cap or blood-gorged crown.

Genetic splendor.

Vigor, spurt of sperm, fecundation.

Perplexity
(scourge of saints)

Wide gullets or truth hard to swallow?
("Guide to the Perplexed")

You gobble down the baited hook
(promise of bitterness to come).

You take communion blindly.
Before you, back gracefully arched
the ever-repeated enigma.

(*Colophon*)

The successive versions, copies, and excisions of the collection of poems all lead me to think that whatever historical material comes down to us is nothing but tawdry lies, trafficking in truth, manipulation. What will the chroniclers say of the siege of this city fifteen centuries from now?*

Missive from D. K. to S. O. S. Sepharad

The Spanish major assigned to this city—who, like all his compatriots of the high command with headquarters in M. who occasionally visit us, shows sympathy with and understanding of the work of the Jewish Humanitarian, Cultural, and Educational Society—personally handed me the sealed envelope that you people dropped off at the ministry a week ago. We have also received via the airlift the third shipment of food and medicines that you informed me of and are awaiting the arrival of the fourth in the next few days unless, as often happens, the besiegers' artillery bombardments of the runways at the airport make it necessary to interrupt the flights and deepen the gloom and worsen the penury in which we live. In the present circumstances, the solidarity and vigilance of S. O. S. Sepharad is more necessary than ever.

Since autumn and the first snowfalls, the situation has continued to worsen. The city does not receive even a fifth of the aid that it cannot do without. I will be frank and forthright: the European Community foists off on us its surpluses and unsalable reserve stocks of food and clothing with no concern for the fact that the siege goes on and on. The barbarians who bomb the city from the hills and take careful aim at women and children in particular want to destroy this little Jerusalem just as those whom they take as their model destroyed Toledo. Several dozen of our brothers who refused to leave here have recently placed their names on the new list of candidates for evacuation. Yesterday mortar shells fell on our neighborhood: the day when the artillerymen perfect their aim and fire on those lined up for the free medicines distributed by our pharmacy, the slaughter will be worse than the ones that, temporarily and hypocritically, "deeply moved" public opinion in the early days of the siege. Two old men belonging to our community passed away last week: one of them died of natural causes and the other of a heart attack brought on by the explosion of a grenade nearby.

As you well know, it is not even possible for us to be buried according to the rites of our religion. The cemetery is on the front line, and the besiegers profaned it by digging their trenches along it.

On a separate sheet, I enclose the list of brothers who are signed up to leave in the next convoy, with their first and last names, ages, and other personal identification. In addition, I enclose a detailed list of the medicines that we are in most urgent need of. The stocks of flour, cooking oil, and vegetables have diminished to dangerous levels and we will be forced to end the distribution of soup if new supplies do not arrive soon.

I shall now broach a delicate subject that has left me perplexed: among the documents having to do with the humanitarian aid and activities of S. O. S. Sepharad that were delivered to us was an envelope sent by someone with an Arab name. I opened it in the belief that it was a report from a brother in Morocco, only to find to my surprise three esoteric texts or "dreams," messianic visions like the one that circulated widely more than 300 years ago in Smyrna, intermingled with astrological themes and erotic hallucinations foreign to our orthodoxy. If, on the one hand, they bear a resemblance to the popular Sufism of the Maghreb, they also call to mind the poems of Eliecer Ben Jonon and the sexual pleasure extolled in thirteenth-century Kabbalistic circles. I do not know whether the sender or author of these texts—someone who signs himself Ben Sidi Abu al-Makârim—is using a pseudonym or whether he is an affiliate of our community.

Intrigued by the oddity of the case, I took advantage of a few hours when things were calm to go to the residence of the leaders and officers of the International Mediation Force and there learned a sad piece of news: the major has been granted sick leave and has been admitted to the base hospital of the organization in Italy; I do not know whether it was because of a sudden illness or a temporary mental aberration. His departure, in any event, is a loss to us, in view of his unusual sensitivity to the problems and hardships of the community. May whoever replaces him share his altruism and his spirit of solidarity!

I would be most grateful to you if you would seek further information concerning this Ben Sidi Abu al-Makârim, in whose dreams there is an unexpected convergence of the mystic and pagan traditions observed by the faithful of the three religions of the Book.

II. BEN SIDI ABU AL-MAKÂRIM

1.

The day the library burned—the target of choice for the brutes who are launching missiles at us and know only sterile hatred—was worse than death. The disappearance of a beloved or even of a member of my immediate family would not have been as bitter a pill for me to swallow. The soul of the city and the more than twenty years of personal research symbolized in that building went up in smoke. From the other side of the river, unable to cross the bridge by order of the firemen who were vainly attempting to put out the fire, I watched in utter despair as the flames devoured it: tongues of flame shooting out the windows, crackling of this furnace fanned by the wind, crashing down of the central lantern, deafening collapse of the walls and ceilings of archives and reading rooms housing thousands of Ottoman, Persian, and Arabic manuscripts. The rage and pain I felt in those moments will follow me to my grave: the treasure destroyed in a few hours included works of history and geography; travel books; philosophy, theology, and Sufism; dictionaries, grammars and analects; treatises on astrology, chess, and music. The objective of the agressors—to leave no trace of the historical substance of this country so as to build on it a temple of lies, legends, and myths—wounded us to the quick. Our collective past and memory, my own life as a researcher in the archives where I found supporting documents and new sources for my research, were reduced to ashes. Even the obsessive memory of the girl turned into a living torch, running about on the first day of the slaughter, howling like one condemned to hell, did not overcome me with the same intensity as those images of ruin and desolation.

"Although you may burn the paper, you will be unable to burn the message written on it because I bear it within my heart," a Moorish poet and philosopher from Andalusia said to the inquisitors who condemned his life's work to the fire; but what heart has room enough to contain the memory of an entire people? All my notebooks, index cards, and glosses on the relations of the Ottoman religious brotherhoods with their counterparts in the Maghreb were lost forever, immolated on the altar of the merciless flames. Today all that is left of the library to which I offered up the best of my life is the hollow shell of its four façades decorated with columns, horseshoe arches, rose windows, and crenels. There where the missiles pierced the metal framework of the roof, it looks like a monstrous spiderweb; the arcades of the inner patio show almost no trace of their former delicate plaster moldings; in the center of the patio is a huge pile of debris, rubble, beams, charred furnishings. This time those responsible for this auto-da-fé burned both paper and the message written on it. A smoke as thick as that rising from the chimneys of the death camps: history reduced to silent spirals, a sky covered with dense clouds blackened by the cinders of our extinction.

The foreign journalists and members of humanitarian organizations with whom I have occasion to talk every day by virtue of my temporary job as receptionist at the H. I.—after some of the hotel staff fled during the first winter of the siege—cannot understand that our sufferings are not so much physical as moral. I am well aware that I am part of the small group of privileged mortals who eat every day and receive tips in marks, yet even if I shared the lot of the majority of those who live in the capital, the gnawing sadness and despair I feel would not come from the hardships of daily life or from the fact that death lies in wait for us at each moment: they are born of the collapse of a dream, from the destruction of a crossroads of different cultures and stores of knowledge, from the loss of a city that lived confidently and joyously until the fatal strangulation brought on by the siege.

How to explain to the press correspondents and the well-meaning intellectuals and writers who sometimes visit us that my problem and that of many of those besieged does not stem from inadequate food supplies, power cuts, and water shortages, nor even from the lack of contact with the outside world? Their compassion does not penetrate to the hidden nucleus of our suffering: our inner desolation, the shattering of our reason for being, the sacking of our memory now scattered to the four winds. In the words of my good friend D. K., of the Jewish Humanitarian, Cultural, and Educational Society, whom I have sometimes consulted with regard to the concept of sanctity among the people of the Maghreb because he is well versed in Ladino, the language of the Jews in Turkey, and the Sephardic adaptations in the Balkans of our Spanish collection of ballads: "You now know, alas, in your own flesh, what fell to our lot to live when we took refuge here, bringing with us the *Haggadah.* Now dispossession and misfortune have made us equals."

These reflections, inspired by the accumulation of incidents and episodes straight out of a novel that have taken place in the last few days, are nonetheless necessary if we are to understand these events. I have no knowledge of the content of the reports submitted by the Spanish major serving with the International Mediation Force, but I can make a good guess as to what was in them in view of my participation in the matter of the death and disappearance of a man who was presumably a fellow country-man of his. I was the one who escorted the major to the room hit by the mortar shell and pretended to be astonished when he discovered that his compatriot's corpse had been stolen or whisked away. I will admit straightway that I did not act alone: the entire staff of the hotel, the medical examiner, and even the official sent by the Presidential Ministry of the Interior to shed light on the mystery collaborated either actively or by omission in this subterfuge. But let us begin at the beginning and not build the house starting with the roof.

On January 4 of last year, the eve of the worst day of the siege, a bearded man around sixty years old turned up at the reception desk, dressed in green and wheeling a beige suitcase; he greeted me in Arabic and handed over a Moroccan passport bearing a name that I recognized immediately: Ben Sidi Abu al-

Makârim, a saint from the capital of the Almohads who was the subject of my research project that went up in smoke in the fire that destroyed the library. His first name, which also appeared on the first page of the passport, was Yahya. Pleasantly surprised by this coincidence, I asked him whether he was one of the saint's descendants or shared in his *baraka*—his miraculous grace. In a heavy accent that clearly indicated his country of origin, he told me that he lived almost in the saint's shadow, in a narrow street near the little hermitage in which his remains repose: opposite a movie theater, he added, that at one time was a slave market. Although his journey had apparently left him exhausted—he had dashed, on foot with his baggage, all the way from the tunnel dug underneath the airport to the hotel, a long and extremely dangerous route—he showed great interest in my references to his native city and the devotion of its people to its Seven Saints. I helped him take his suitcase up to the fifth floor and left him in his room after making certain that he had candles and a flashlight. Dinner is served at seven, I added as I started down the corridor. That was the first and last time I saw him alive.

On returning to the reception desk, I leafed through the passport so as to record his name in the guest register. My growing impression that it was a false one became even stronger once the generator came back on and I had carefully examined it. Whether or not it was an authentic document, the information added by hand was written over a different name and surname like a palimpsest. The embossed stamp on top of his photograph on the third page likewise struck me as being a forgery. Nor did I find an entry visa for any of the neighboring countries. Had he managed to cross borders and get past the checkpoints set up to intercept bandits and outlaws without being detected? Even granting that such an improbable hypothesis was true, the reason for his journey through the inferno of war and ethnic cleansing remained an enigma. What was a man like him, who had nothing whatsoever to do with the conflict, doing here in this human trap, jam-packed with so many suffering souls? Was he a double or a lookalike of the saint buried in the hermitage, or had he come here to meet his death, knowing its exact place and time?

I was hoping to see him in the dining room on the mezzanine, but he didn't show up. I was tempted to take his dinner upstairs to him on a tray, but I gave up the idea: he was no doubt fast asleep. I decided to put off our meeting again till the following day and ran, as I did every night, zigzagging like a hare that knows it is being tracked by invisible rifles with night sights, to my miserable lair in the old city: a building charred on the outside, in whose insides the victims of the reign of terror, its sorely tried guinea pigs, had taken shelter.

The artillery bombardment the next morning found me back at the hotel. Safe and sound in the apse of the immense crypt, I listened to the din of the volleys, landing close at hand at first and then right inside the great empty shell that, like a bunker, resists the assaults of the enemy war machine, its stubborn, vicious harassment. The few windowpanes still in one piece along the staircase came crashing down: the same artillery shell destroyed the abandoned dining room. Seconds later, another shell exploded on the fifth floor, in the part of it in which the real or supposed Ben Sidi Abu al-Makârim was staying. I waited, crouched down behind the reception desk, till the artillerymen wearied of bombing us and chose another target. With a colleague from the university sent to keep the H. I.'s accounts and one of the soldiers assigned to guard duty at the hotel, I went up to the room that had been hit by a mortar shell. A Dutch diplomat lodged in another wing on the same floor also wanted to see the damage, and his ill-fated intrusion—he was by nature a booby-bird who stuck his beak in everywhere—complicated my plans, as we shall see. Without him, things would have been much simpler: neither my friends nor I would have been obliged to even mention the corpse! But with his clumsy stride of a long-legged stork, he followed us to the room.

The traveler who had arrived the night before lay stretched out on the floor on his back. A curiously serene expression illuminated his face. The beige suitcase was still closed, but a bound notebook, lying on the bed, had escaped any damage from the shelling. I hurriedly picked it up: the typed title, *Astrolabe*, had another, directly underneath, written by hand: *In the Shadow of Sidi Abu al-Makârim*. How to describe my emotion as I leafed through the pages of it? It was as though I were reading my own work! The verses coincided word for word with the ones I had copied out in my dissertation! My hands trembled and my gaze was arrested by the page whose epigraph read: "Reading of Sidna Alí in the Patio of S. A. F.":

You call to mind empires fallen to ruin, devastated dwellings, the
     slow decrepitude of corrupt people
everything they did while they lived and had power
what they achieved, how they went to perdition, how they were
     induced to rob and abuse those weaker than they
(their souls took wing, they were left soulless).

Although they may feel firmly established at the summit, in reality
     they are still journeying
their past does not exist
their present will disappear.

Where are those who preceded them in their thirst for power and
     riches?
in the end what did they earn for themselves in their lifetime?
what was their contribution to the light of humanity?

Being a reader familiar with Sufi masters and their disciples and hermit saints revered from Mauritania to Uzbekistan, the signs of his sanctity manifested themselves to me in a lightning flash of blinding revelation. The other compositions of the collection of poems, as well as certain texts of Sidi Ben Slimân al-Jazuli, brought me back to the central theme of my study, to the fruit of twenty years of cruelly destroyed research. The urgency of putting all that in a safe place severely taxed my ingenuity. On pain of being despoiled for the second time of everything that gives meaning to my life, I would have to hide the traveler's corpse and the written proofs of his mission. My colleague from the university and the security guard—a member, like all his family, of the ancient Naqshabandiyy brotherhood—agreed with me. After having brusquely taken leave of the diplomat, we quickly found ourselves of one mind as to the necessity of spiriting away the body of Ben Sidi Abu Al-Makârim before the police began an investigation and of inventing a new identity for the man who had "disappeared," with the valuable help of a former librarian and Hispanist who survives the siege as best he can in his lair on the riverbank opposite the blocks of apartments from which the snipers practice their aim each day, their target of choice being this "safe zone" that has turned into an odd sort of game preserve.

2.

I was giving the finishing touches to a short story entitled "The Mortal Enemy," inspired by my grueling personal experience of the siege, when I received an unexpected visit from my colleague and old companion at times of moving moments, discoveries, and heartache at the research center of the library, presently employed, because of his knowledge of some twenty languages, as a receptionist at the poor battered H. I.

Our friendship, based on affinities and shared interests, goes back more than three decades: both of us have a passion for languages and a weakness for word games and tongue twisters. In the happy days before the war we used to carry on mock arguments, switching from one language to another on the spur of the moment: I would speak to him, for example, in Spanish and he would reply in Arabic; if I attacked him in Turkish, he would answer me back in Farsi. The library was our favorite haunt: it was there that we discussed the realm of the divine and the human, went from the esotericism of Ibn al-'Arabi to the initiatory chain of the Ottoman brotherhoods, from the grandeur and decadence of the corps of janissaries and renegade Christians who served the sultan to the variants of the traditional Ladino collection of ballads through the centuries and the life and miracles of the patron saints and holy men of the medina in Marrakesh. Since we were living index card files, we would meet once the library closed in one of the taverns near the river, sometimes accompanied by the musician D. K. of the Jewish Humanitarian, Cultural, and Educational Society, and stimulated by the bottle of wine promptly set before us, each of us would pit our erudition and knowledge against that of the other as the conversation touched on the religious syncretism of the Macedonian Bektachi or the literary and philosophical exchanges between the Maghreb and al Andalus in the era of the Almoravids. Often we continued our polyglot jousts in the street—we were fond of following words from Arabia to Spain, tracing, for instance, the Mediterranean journey of the term *kafir, gavur, guarí, guiri* in its meaning of infidel or barbarian—and would end the evening, happy and a bit tipsy, with a ritual visit to the monastery of Hadji Sinane, the refuge of the Qadiriyya brotherhoods during the religious persecution they suffered at the hands of the disciples of orthodoxy.

Whereas I have always been drawn to literature, my friend's great love has been history: he was preparing a major work on the unknown or half-forgotten saints of the capital of the Almohads and regularly exchanged letters on the subject with the chroniclers of that city. He was the victim of far worse luck than I. I had kept my manuscripts and notes at home, but the burning of the library by the pyromaniacs who were laying siege to us had reduced to ashes every last one of his documents and files: an entire lifetime suddenly gone up in smoke.

Isolated from each other because of the bombings and the fury of the snipers, we have seen each other only very infrequently after the disaster. Going outside on the street to get firewood or food is an adventure in the course of which you risk your neck: either we dash out to the places where water is available and food is distributed or else we stay cloistered at home. That is why his venturing out to my neighborhood surprised me and overjoyed me. The siege of the city does not encourage this sort of visit: of the long list of hardships we suffer from, loneliness may well be the worst.

My friend loomed up in the semidarkness of the stairwell like a ghost. We exchanged a fervent embrace. To protect himself from the cold and the snow he was wearing rubber boots and a thick parka inside which his thin, frail body floated like a scarecrow. The besiegers bestowed a shower of shells upon us and the explosions followed one after the other without a letup. How had he dared come to my place, only 200 meters away from the enemy, if it were not for a crucial, urgent reason?

He: I needed to speak with you immediately and ask for your help! For me, today is the happiest day of the siege!

I: are you touched in the head?

He: yes, touched by grace, luck, or whatever you care to call it. What I lost in the fire at the library has been returned to me!

(Was he having a fit of madness? I decided to talk to him in paternal tones.)

I: well then, do tell me about it. But we can talk better inside this cubbyhole that I use as an office.

He: it's fantastic! Do you know who turned up yesterday at the H. I.? One of those saints who were the subject of my doctoral dissertation!

I: I thought that the youngest of them had passed away several hundred years ago!

He: Ben Sidi Abu al-Makârim!

I: it must have been a descendant of his!

He: a descendant or a reincarnation, what difference does it make? The important thing is that he's part of the *sîlsîla,* the initiatory chain! You surely know, don't you, that the *baraka* is hereditary among them?

I: and he's staying at the hotel?

He: he was a while ago!

I: and now he's left?

He: he died just this morning! A mortar shell made a direct hit on his room!

I: are you sure you're not dreaming?

He: I'd have the same reaction as you if you handed *me* a story like that! Look at this notebook with his poems! He brought it with him in the suitcase and that's why I've come to see you! It must be put in a good safe place!

I went to the kitchen to make him a cup of coffee. He waited impatiently for me, standing next to the little table with my manuscripts piled up on top of it, and when I came back with the tray, he opened a little folder that he was holding.

He: read this page with me! You'll see whether I'm touched in the head or not!

3. Almanac Page

From the intimate nocturnal intertwining to the propriety of morning, listening intently to the polyphonic voices that rend the air as dawn peeks its eyebrow over the horizon: the prayer of the muezzin that traces the borderline between the luminous Night of the mystics and the Dark Zenith of a star that deals mercilessly with those who dwell in the city. No human event disturbs the implacable routine of the solar cycles, the drama and the majesty of their eternal repetition. The theophanies of the Seven Holy Men form part of an inner landscape: they are not accessible to the profane. Visitors do not know their secret story, womb of another story: this one invisible, spiritual.

You are on your way to the public square, the still-empty space of the square. Those who have slept out of doors wake up and stretch; the cafés open; tenuous signs of life appear. Twelve hours later, as the day draws to a close and the bleeding sun sets, the knots of the curious who gather and disperse will turn this space into a vast stage setting where multiple plots and intrigues that vary from day to day are played out.

Like the solitary man amid the multitude described to us by Ibn al-'Arabi—for whom a crowd was a hermit's retreat and the desert a public square—you settle down comfortably in the corner café, from which idle onlookers can watch, for free, the improvised spectacle of their lives.

In honor of the great global marketplace about to open, the square has been paved, decorated, swept clean, and its public chased out at the end of a broom: a wise old woman decked out as a young bride. But the river of life returns to its bed: the jugglers have come back, the kitchens are giving off smoke, the women who sell bread are squatting on their heels beneath their tutelary umbrellas. What was lost on a Monday is found again on a Tuesday. No municipal ordinance can prevail in the face of cunning and tenacity. What better symbol of their ineffectiveness than uniformed policemen?: the moment they appear on the scene pullovers, trousers, toys, wool caps disappear as if by magic, only to reappear just as swiftly the minute their backs are turned. Authority that imposes itself only to be canceled out: does this not embody the fleeting nature of all power? Xemáa el Fná is an effective antidote against the fiction of history: supposedly eternal empires and laws that nonetheless vanish without a trace like a nomad's footprints.

For three consecutive days on your way to the square you come upon a tiny, starving, abandoned kitten. You have hoped in vain for a charitable soul to come by to help: the fellow members of its species, more battle-hardened, wage ferocious fights over the refuse in the garbage cans, yet no one takes pity on it. Finally, its forlornness touches your heart: has this bald, mangy little cat, so cruelly branded by every imaginable misery, been born only to suffer? You solicitously bring it a bowl of milk, the leftovers from a stew, and watch its tentative lapping, its avid mastication, its first experience of something that has nothing to do with pain or hardship.

Its image has accompanied you in your retreat amid the crowd, from which you observe its continual, fecund hustle and bustle. On your way home, you are not surprised to come across the creature's dead body, skinny and hairless but with a full round belly; it died, people tell you, from overeating. A strange sensation electrifies you: at least it has known happiness for a few minutes; its inert little body justifies the act that created it. The prayer at twilight silences the square, drums and castanets no longer sound, birds retire to their nests, spaces teeming with life are suddenly empty. From the terrace you witness the interiorization of the light. The space throbs with hidden life.

BEN SIDI ABU AL-MAKÂRIM

4.

I allowed myself to be contaminated by the madness of the grammarians of whom Erasmus speaks. The mystic content of the collection of poems and the name of their author in all truth justified my friend's excitement. What did it matter whether or not the man who called himself Ben Sidi Abu al-Makârim was the saint himself, whether his descendant or double had defied the horror of the siege and sacrificed his life as a definite, irrefutable proof?

The last poem in the notebook left no doubt as to his place in the initiatory chain of those *auliya* who scorn conventions, act with no inhibitions, and choose to renounce life rather than cling to a sterile and unrewarding old age.

In your mad race against time
(few grains of sand are now left in the top of the hourglass)
you devote yourself to more and more travels, escapes, advances,
orgasms, dangers.

In search of the bullet that will mow you down?
or of a writing that also escapes you and slips between your
fingers?

Death and decrepitude are everywhere around you.
How to avoid erosion with dignity?

We would have to cook up a plan then and there to spirit away the corpse along with its false papers and then secretly bury it among the *almocadenes* and spiritual guides laid to rest in the cemetery of Alifakovac. To do so, my friend said, we could count on the connivance of the hotel staff as well as on our good friend F. K., the medical examiner, who before the siege had regularly joined our little circle of polyglots when we met. As we worked out our project and the conversation grew more animated, we recovered all our old exuberance and sense of humor. Victims of this medieval siege, so like the one endured by the Albigensians, we resolved to fight back on our own by means of a stratagem that was also medieval: the dissemination of texts, for in that period a glorious coterie of copyists, clerks, interpreters, monks of scant virtue, and wayward young scholar-poets distributed throughout the monasteries and centers of learning of the era theories, commentaries, sophistic arguments, interpolations, and apocrypha that undermined the certainties and dogmas of the Church, the eternal aspiration of power to centralize thought in order to render it toothless and tame.

During my most recent stay in Spain, where I was invited to the Congress of Comparative Literatures that had met in Barcelona two months before the siege, a very close friend, with whom I share many tastes and pleasures that we cannot always admit to, offered me as a gift a collection of poems that he had bought in a secondhand stall, assuring me with a conspiratorial air that its contents were bound to interest me. According to what he told me, he had turned up the official, confidential records of the archives of the psychiatric hospital of the stronghold of M., in North Africa, in the street stall of a junk dealer in the city buried amid a pile of old objects and utensils. The volumes for sale included the personal history, the medical diagnosis, and the dates of admission and release from the hospital of some thousand patients sent there during the Spanish civil war and the implacable repression that ensued. Those confined in the asylum, many of them for political reasons or ideological deviationism, were classified in the records of the psychiatrists as suffering from idiocy, feeblemindedness, senility, homosexuality, insanity, intermittent melancholia, and persecution mania. The patient listed only by his initials, "J. G.," and characterized as "an inveterate sodomite, a pervert and a schizophrenic" had been admitted to the center on July 19, 1936, and had escaped six months later with the help of a soldier from the Tabor, in the French zone of the Protectorate, where all trace of the two of them, their records add succinctly, was completely lost. The little notebook with a green cover, consisting of six pages each corresponding to a text whose length and meter differed, bore in the margins the scrawls of a very specific category of readers: comments and phrases insulting the soldiers, psychiatrists, and chaplains who ruled over that sinister prison disguised as a hospital.

Placing the poems of "J. G." among these documents would bewilder the investigators and put them on a false trail: we had only to give Ben Sidi Abu al-Makârim a Spanish-sounding name and turn him into the unknown author of the verses bought at the junk dealer's stall for the matter to fall under the jurisdiction of the major of that nationality in charge of civil affairs at the high command of the International Mediation Force, who would be lost in this hodgepodge of labyrinthian texts carefully and cunningly assembled. My innate antipathy toward the military, grown even stronger in the years of obligatory service in the army of the Federation and its bemedaled and incombustible marshal, had turned to hatred ever since that unforgettable month of April 1992, when, drunk on beer and prayers to their invincible Saint Sava, army troops had shot at peaceful citizens who were theoretically under their protection: as in Spain in 1936, they had declared war on their own people and covered themselves with honor by shedding the innocent blood of their countrymen.

I had once dined with miles gloriosus in the company of a Navarrese internist who was a member of Doctors Without Borders, and the discreet references of the former to the "belligerents" and "parties involved in the conflict" so as to avoid all mention of besiegers and besieged, murderers and victims, infuriated me. By common accord between my friend and colleague and myself, we decided to lay another trap for the major as a special bonus: along with the collection of poems by "J. G.," I would contribute another element to our game: narratives about the siege that were my own handiwork. The very idea of his confusion elated the two of us and we congratulated each other in the twenty-some languages we knew. I have forgotten the customary formula in Urdu!, he sighed. How do you say "far out!" in Tamazigh? We must resuscitate the words that were burned up in the fire and put them back in circulation! Rescue them from the ashes and give them back to our native tongue, to life! It was as though the siege had suddenly ceased and we were again having a lively discussion in our little polyglot circle, as in days gone by.

But there was no time to lose. I began to select stories from the ones I'd already typed up, including the one in which I refer sarcastically to a major of the International Mediation Force and his fictitious reports, and caught up in our prankishness of the old days, we agreed to set one of them aside and send it to "J. G." with the address of a post office box in the Paris neighborhood in which I had lived while I was writing my dissertation. Our so-called saviors not only remain on the sidelines with their arms folded when the snipers kill kids who slip out of their refuges to play in the snow and make piles of money on the black market trafficking in our suffering, but also confiscate the letters that the besieged leave at the reception desk of the H. I. for guests passing through who are willing to serve as postmen. Methodical and punctilious as he is, the major would no doubt rummage through the mail sacks confiscated at the airport in search of clues and trails to follow!

I handed my friend an envelope with my stories and the collection of poems. I have never seen him as excited as he was at that moment. I'm Ben Sidi al-Makârim, and I've inherited his *baraka!,* he kept saying. The rain of shells had emptied the streets of the city, but the risk of returning to the hotel by crossing through the most exposed areas did not seem to worry him. I can find no other way of describing him: he was levitating for joy.

The library has not burned down in vain, he added as we bade each other good-bye in the dim light of the stairwell. Its ashes have fallen on fertile ground and now they will sprout on the saint's tomb!

We were overcome with sheer bliss. We would fight against the enemy and his doctrine of borders traced in blood with the eternal and subtle weapon of the weak: the seminal dispersion of their voices, the infinite variants of the Word!

5.

With my colleagues at the hotel and my old friend the medical examiner, we set out the props in the room destroyed by the mortar shell. We left the notebook with "J. G.'s" poems on the bed, we put my comrade's accounts of the siege in the beige suitcase—I put the fifth one in an envelope addressed to him, as we had agreed—and taking advantage of the yawning holes created by the pounding from the artillery, we transported Ben Sidi Abu al-Makârim's body wrapped in a blanket to the service elevator that by a miracle was working, thanks to the generator. This freight elevator, whose existence the transient guests of the hotel are not aware of, goes straight down to the basement, where part of the official archives of the Republic are piled up in a number of rooms adjoining the dirty, ramshackle parking garage. This time the inquisitive Dutch booby-bird didn't poke his beak in to see what was going on.

The deceased, watched over by a soldier from the Qadiriyya brotherhood who had been put in prison for his beliefs several years earlier, remained there for several hours waiting to be taken to the cemetery of Alifakovac while my colleagues and I did some fancy capework with the Spanish major who had been sent immediately to take care of matters by the high command of the International Mediation Force, just as we had foreseen.

Straightfaced, but laughing up our sleeves, we each played the role we had assumed, making sure that our behavior and gestures conformed to the major's discovery that the traveler's body had disappeared and that all his papers were missing. You should have seen the man's face, his patience already sorely tried by my English that was halting at best, on being confronted with the revelations that followed one upon the other, just as set down in our script! The drawing up of the death certificate by the medical examiner and the statements taken from the person to whom he mistakenly refers to in his report as "a temporary administrator" dragged on until late afternoon.

The security guard and my sister-in-law—who worked with me at the reception desk and put the "lost" passport in a safe place—confirmed our statements and witnessed our signatures. The major was visibly perplexed: the whole affair defied logic and common sense! Finally he left, accompanied by his junior officers, and we escorted them to the white armored car parked outside the side door of the hotel. He announced that he would finish his investigation the following day. In point of fact, his ordeal had only begun.

As soon as the deafening concert of shells and mortar fire had died down, we loaded Ben Sidi Abu al-Makârim's body into a minivan, drove across the city plunged in darkness, past the dead library to the little bridge that crosses the river, and finally reached the road that zigzags its way up the hill to the cemetery. Although hidden at times by clouds, the moon traveled with us all the way. Like Sidi Muhammad de Belcourt and Ibn Turmeda of Tunis, the obscure saint of the capital of the Almohads would rest for all eternity in two tombs: the one in the anonymous hermitage in the Kennaría district and the other a more modest one—a simple stele with the name and the age shown on the passport—in our devastated city. Dr. F. K. had taken care of filing the death certificate, as required by law, at the hospital morgue. As he told me in confidence weeks later, the authorities kept the entire complicated affair quiet, convinced that the presumed Moroccan citizen had come to enlist as a soldier, despite his advanced age, in the corps of forces loyal to the government, described by the Fascists' propaganda as "the poisoned sword of Islam thrust into the heart of the West."

His official death was thus that of a martyr come from a distant country to defend his brothers in danger: deeply moved, we broke the precarious calm of the night by chanting the ritual Prayer for the Absent One.

III. THE MEETING OF THE POLYGLOTS

A.

After the carnage at the central market caused by the explosion of a mortar shell—fired, as certain anonymous spokesmen of the International Mediation Force declared as usual, by the victims of the siege themselves so as to win the pity of the entire world and thereby bring on the aerial bombing so often announced with great fanfare yet never carried out—the situation of the city improved. The intervention of the Western powers so long hoped for did not take place—God or Godot never turned up, as in the play put on several months before by candlelight in the badly damaged little experimental theater—but the heavy artillery pieces with which the city was bombarded day after day temporarily moved a few kilometers farther way after an interchange of several shows of force between the besiegers and the multinational command that were nothing but bluster. S. woke up one fine morning without the usual broadside of shells and grenades. The city's inhabitants cautiously emerged from their lairs in search of firewood, food, and water, not daring to really believe in this unexpected stroke of luck. The snow-covered hills and mountains looked clean and polished, as though wearing a mask of feigned innocence. Even the snipers posted in the buildings on the other side of the river gave evidence of a strange moderation and abstained from practicing their aim on women and children. The siege went on, but the rope around the necks of the city's people had been loosened. Magnanimously, the urbicides allowed them to gulp in a few breaths of air, lying in wait for the moment when a favorable set of circumstances would permit them to strangle them again so as to bring on their last panting death rattle.

Although brief and fortuitous, the truce restored a semblance of life to the city. People went on pushing their wheelbarrows loaded with jerricans and standing in line at the food distribution centers, but they no longer crossed dangerous intersections in terror or desperately hugged the barriers of containers and freight cars set up for their protection. Little by little, a few cafés opened up again and those lucky enough to have foreign currency met in them to exchange memories of the vicissitudes and horrors of the siege. A visit to the cemetery was no longer an act of courage: the besieged gathered in them in droves to pray and place flowers on the graves of their relatives and friends.

Our old acquaintances also emerged from their respective lairs. Like marmots at the end of a long winter, they defied the cold and the snow that still covered the streets to meet in a café on the rubbish-strewn Avenue of the Marshal, in the shelter of the arches of an old porte cochère. The place was lighted by just one small kerosene lamp. Crowded around its tables, the customers, wearing caps and fur hats, looked more like smugglers or conspirators.

The historian who worked as a desk clerk at the H. I. and the author of the accounts of the siege that had so upset the major began their polyglot meetings again, by themselves at first and then later with other members. The mere fact of having survived that inferno strengthened the bonds of the intellectual complicity that they had so sorely missed. Gradually, other companions who had diligently frequented the defunct library but had dropped out of sight since the beginning of the siege began to join them. Dr. F. K., the medical examiner from the hospital, also came after work, together with the Navarrese internist from Doctors Without Borders. After twenty months of an institutionalized nightmare, they reacted to events with wit and humor. To begin with, they invented different nicknames for the main characters and the extras who had played a part in the drama:

Slobe Globe
Milo Venusevic
Elvenus Milo-Chechnik
The Bardobomber
Kara's Schtick

Shakesnipear
De Lors be praised
Smile Made in Japon
Minus Major
Mutter Rand
General Morpheon
Peter Peter-Cheap

and they then translated them into every known language and orchestrated the variants in a sort of fiercely jocose Esperanto. It was a way of limbering up their brains, stretching the muscles of their wit, preparing themselves to withstand the new trials with which they would inexorably be confronted. Nonetheless, their worries and anxieties stemmed from different causes, and once the first days of euphoria were past, they rose like oil spots to the surface of the water: the circle of polyglots turned into a circle of detectives. Each member thought he had a clue or was in possession of the key to the enigma. The wine from the coast flowed freely: the clerk at the reception desk of the H. I. took it upon himself to pay the tab thanks to the tips in marks and dollars he received from the humanitarian tourists who, as he put it cynically, "come here on a sight-seeing trip, to pity our sufferings and photograph them."

B. Who Was Ben Sidi Abu al-Makârim?

The question tormented me, and once I began pondering the mystery of his visit, the contradictions and anachronisms mounted, my doubts became more numerous, and my perplexity more profound. In the months before the siege I had exchanged letters concerning his forebear with the chroniclers of the capital of the Almohads. The data gleaned by H. T. and Si M. K. regarding the saint—which had disappeared along with the remainder of my documents and notes in the fire that destroyed the library—were notable only for their scarcity and brevity. The only verses extant that were written in his own hand are copies of those of his long-ago master in Konya: be a slave and tread the ground as the horse does. Do not seek to rise on the backs of the people and hence be like the corpse being carried off to the cemetery. In later analects, in all likelihood apocryphal, the anonymous compiler praises his mordant criticism of the powerful and emphasizes the unusual lesson in humility he taught: defecating in public as the supreme demonstration of the equality of all creatures and their submission to the universal order of the Cosmos. For this reason certain adversaries of his doctrine are said to have called him "the Defecator," hoping to discredit him in the eyes of his followers, but "he had learned to swallow his pride and seek his perfection within himself." According to the chroniclers with whom he corresponded, other testimony of his contemporaries alludes to him in passing, mentions his charisma and his renown, but says nothing about the contents of his lost mystical writings.

Was the collection of poems brought with him by the dead man a modernized transcription of these latter works or the exclusive product of his imagination? The many liberties taken with chronology and the references that did not correspond to the practice and the learning of his era tipped the scales in favor of the second hypothesis. The author's supposed fund of Latin and Hispanic knowledge does not accord with what was known of the holy man buried in the hermitage of Riad Zeitún. Although it was perhaps possible to trace the initiatory chain back to the *malamatí,* the illuminati and visionaries close to the esotericism of Ibn al- ʿArabi and Mawlana, the quotations from Plautus and the author of *La Celestina* were obviously incongruous and absurd: the break with the historical substratum, created by osmosis and decantations, out of which European culture arose had become a reality two centuries before, thanks to the men of the Renaissance and the gradual extinction of Western Islam.

In my intuitive approach to the lost work of the saint, I had written poems that coincided verse for verse with those copied out in the collection of poems. That is what I told my old friend and fellow Hispanicist who had been trapped for months in his apartment on the riverbank, although I did not succeed in entirely convincing him. Since the originals had been reduced to ashes, might my recollections of them not be the result of a posterior mental reconstruction? The impossibility of placing my poems side by side with those of Ben Sidi Abu al-Makârim and comparing them served to justify his skepticism. But there remained the fact, to me undeniable, that I could still feel the pain it had caused me to write them down; I made them as much a part of myself as though they were my own; I assumed their paternity. I could recite them to him from memory, the one entitled "Candelabrum for Tenebrae" for example, that I had composed in my beloved haunt, the now-vanished library, in a state of fusion—of confusion, he corrected me—with my spiritual double:

The grace of the Word transpierces you, illuminates you, takes you
back to your aridities.

Swift flashes, barely set alight before they are extinguished, cause
of abjection and perplexity.

Opacity, unsureness, brevity of the gift.

You leaf through, listlessly, sterile pages of your dictionary.

The opening verses of the notebook likewise matched word for word what I had written, guided by an illumination or a presentiment: I could swear to him by all I hold most dear that I was not making the whole thing up, nor was I the victim of a hallucination! Yet he stood his ground and grabbed the little notebook out of my hands.

And what about this poem? Did you compose it before the siege too?

(I reread the one entitled "Full Stop"—that I had shown him on the very morning that I discovered the dead body in the hotel room—and despite myself had to admit that I hadn't.)

Listen. There is a pseudo Sidi Abu al-Makârim as there was a pseudo Denys the Areopagite. Your manuscripts have been tampered with!

Then who is the Arab who brought them and contacted me? You can't make me believe that we met by chance and that he wasn't sent by someone!

Someone? Who? Aren't our destinies written? Ask God that question, or if you prefer, the compiler of the book!

(The kerosene in the lamp was all gone. We were left in the dark. As the owner of the dive came over to refill it, lighting his way with a cigarette lighter, we prudently changed the subject.)

C.

If doubts assailed my colleague concerning the existence and poetic works of Ben Sidi Abu al-Makârim, similar doubts gnawed at me regarding the author of *Sotadic Zone.*

What name was hidden behind the enigmatic "J. G.," confined for sodomy and moral depravity to the psychiatric hospital of M. by the military officers who had staged the coup?

Could the verses, whose rough language was closer to the sadomasochistic experience of habitués of leather bars than to the modesty and nostalgia of a Cernuda or a Cavafy, have been written half a century ago, and more inconceivable still, in the asphyxiating climate of a fort governed by chaplains and officers whose dreams of a crusade and plans of salvation for the Fatherland anticipated those being invoked today by the besiegers to justify our extermination?

The bare facts regarding the admission and flight from that madhouse or prison of one of the few who miraculously escaped the kangaroo court and the common grave of those executed in the great cleansing were all that I had to go on: everything else remained shrouded in fog. Where and when was he born, what was his profession, who were the soldiers and husky, robust young men he extolled in his verses, how did he manage to escape and find refuge on the other side of the border, only to vanish in the end without a trace with his lover and accomplice from the Moroccan Tabor Corps? Did the initials "J. G." stand for his real name or had they been inserted with the intention of confusing readers as to his identity? The Latin glosses and barbed remarks in the margins lent credence to the suspicion that hoodwinking was involved: the secret intervention of a multitude of copyists, commentators, authors of interpolations and glosses that were superimposed and interwoven so as to deliberately complicate all access to the original. Was there a pseudo J. G., as there had no doubt been a pseudo Sidi Abu al-Makârim? I felt like a fly trapped in a very finely woven textual spiderweb.

The Navarrese internist from Doctors Without Borders added new elements to this uncertainty: the little notebook with a green cover found in the major's room in the residence of junior and senior officers of the International Mediation Force was not identical to the one that I had entrusted to my friend and colleague, the desk clerk at the H. I. The major appeared to have added more insults and crossed out with a pen the paragraphs that shocked him! According to his testimony, the first poems in the notebook had been mutilated or torn out altogether. Only four verses remained of the one entitled "The Potter." Of "The Body Guard," two. As for "Mystery Play"—suppressed in its entirety—it had apparently been replaced with another page containing the Christian Credo and several lines from the Bible concerning the divine punishment of Sodom. The major must have devoured the originals in a fit of madness before falling into a profound catalepsy and being secretly evacuated to an allied military base!

But when the Navarrese mentioned a satirical gloss on the declarations of the current president of the Spanish Conference of Bishops and the reproduction, in a footnote, of a thesis having to do with the sexual abstinence of priests as a violation of the natural order, condemned along with 218 other heretical propositions by the University of Paris in 1277—intercalations that were not in the notebook that had come into my hands— my bewilderment and disbelief knew no bounds. The marginal annotation could perhaps be attributed to an obsession on the part of the major or a split personality, but how to bridge the gap between the knowledge of medieval theology and Latin erudition displayed in the footnote and the figure of a mere regular army officer, an average, run-of-the-mill product of a typical military academy?

To my question, posed at one of the evening meetings of our polyglot circle, he answered with an ambiguous pleasantry: we philologists are capable of anything! Don't forget that I was responsible for the inventory of his effects—I was the only one of his compatriots that was available—and, naturally, no one kept watch on me as I drew it up!

Although that gave us a good laugh and we exchanged jokes about the major's tribulations, my impression that he had spoken the truth grew stronger once I was by myself and had a chance to think about it. If I had had no difficulty slipping my stories of the siege into the beige suitcase of the pseudo J. G. with the connivance of my friend the desk clerk, who could guarantee that the Navarrese pacifist, impelled by his horror of genocide and the international failure to act, had not tried his hand at a similar game and slyly appended a cryptic signature?

Nonetheless, the problems raised by the collection of poems did not end there: the notebook with the green cover bought at the junk dealer's street stall lacked a title! Was I certain of that? my friend and colleague the desk clerk had asked, visibly upset. As certain as I am of being who I am, I said to him: the title *Sotadic Zone* had been added later. On this score I was absolutely certain and the historical circumstances supported it: although the works of the writer who coined that expression— Richard Burton, the author of an excellent account of the Muslim pilgrimage to Mecca—today enjoy a certain renown in Spain, he was completely unknown at the time that the verses were written. The possibility that J. G. had had access to his books must be discounted. If someone gave the collection of poems that title it was after the unforgettable morning of the artillery bombardment and the death of Ben Sidi Abu al-Makârim.

To shed light on the enigma, I questioned the Navarrese internist as we drained our glasses of wine before the sounding of the nightly curfew broke up our little gathering.

Was it you or the major?

He was definitely the one, he answered. I give you my word as a medievalist, with a doctorate cum laude in philology!

D.

When they let up the siege that was choking the life out of us so as to use their smoke-and-mirror tricks and give us the illusion of a semblance of a normal existence, I continued to keep my ears pricked up for the least sound of barbarism, crouching in the mountains where the maker of myths inspired by the muse of poetry and wearing a psychiatrist's white smock was sharpening, is sharpening still, his bloody butcher knife.

This is where I have a definite advantage over the others: while the horrors of war and ethnic cleansing had taken them by surprise, my brothers and I are experiencing once again hardships that go back centuries: diasporas, forced conversions, autos-da-fé, stigmata of infamy, the work of a clergy hardened by the battle against the Moors and a populace of simon-pure blood whose hatred of learning and letters led it to glorify illiteracy as the supreme proof of its ancestral heritage! Our expulsion and our wandering, first through Italy and then along the Dalmatian coast, eventually came to an end in this Ottoman city, hospitable haven and fertile crucible of cultures. We arrived here with our precious *Haggadah*, a treasure so many times banished and hidden, the symbol of our millenary faith, of our incurable nostalgia for our lost home. Experience has taught us that no progress of civilization is lasting, that exclusivism and intolerance mine it from within, that pogroms and ethnic cleansings take place again and again. Patterns of coexistence, well-being, and spirituality that appear to be well established can collapse overnight. That is what happened in Sepharad to the greater glory of their Catholic Majesties; that is what is happening today in this martyrized and dying little Jerusalem.

Once I had regained my freedom of movement, confiscated along with so many other things by those who rained shells down on us each day, my first visit was to the offices of the presidency, where the vice rector of the university officially informed me that the *Haggadah* had been miraculously preserved from the flames that destroyed the museum in which it had been hidden. I have never been so deeply moved nor doubtless will I ever be again: the manuscript, saved from the Nazis by our Muslim friends, had escaped yet again the fire set ablaze by those who are endeavoring to avenge affronts centuries old—the loss of the kingdom to the Turks, the death of Prince Lazar, the defeat on the Field of Blackbirds—venting their cruelty on a patrimony that defies their fables! A professor from the university had identified the book in the basement of the building and since then it has been securely stored away in a vault in the National Bank.

My joy, and that of our minuscule community, defies all written expression: we weep, we offer prayers of thanksgiving, we embrace each other, we make our way from hardness of heart and meanness of spirit to the fervor of an authentic and imperishable faith that has found fulfillment.

I had entirely lost touch with my friends in the circle of polyglots and wanted to pass the good news on to them. According to what I heard from someone working with the Benevolensiya, they now meet late in the afternoon in a little café near the covered market to fight the hardships and gloom of the siege with the subtle weapons of erudition and humor. They greeted me in all the languages I know and some I don't: in Spanish and Hebrew, Arabic and Esperanto, happy to have me back with them and see with their own eyes that all of us were still alive. Then we raised our glasses in a toast in honor of the *Haggadah*. A few bits of our common memory had been saved from barbarism: Karaschtick had not had his own way altogether!

The conversation finally turned to the Spanish major of the International Mediation Force and his sudden sick leave. The scholar doing research on popular sanctity in the Maghreb and the writer trapped for months in his apartment on the river's edge told me all about the visit and the death of Ben Sidi Abu al-Makârim and the replacement of his passport and his manuscripts. I listened to them in silence as they talked about the poetry inspired by the holy man, and about the enigmatic J. G. and his verses. The main theme of the collection of poems—a frank and uninhibited homosexuality—seemed to coincide with that of the "First Dream," which the poor major had given me along with the mail for S. O. S. Sepharad. Although the addressee's name was missing on the envelope, this was mere negligence on the part of the sender: in answer to my questions, the secretary of our sister association explained that his letter of introduction had gone astray and the envelope was being sent, at the request of an acquaintance of his, to the writer and Hispanicist who belonged to our polyglot circle. My words upset those present: the person in question and the historian of Ben Sidi Abu al-Makârim as well and even the young Navarrese internist from Doctors Without Borders showed signs of anxiety and discomposure. After they had exchanged a look of such distress that it disconcerted me, the former took the bull by the horns.

He: if I am not mistaken, you said that the envelope was addressed to me.

I: precisely. It contains three "Dreams" written in the second person with allusions to the siege, apocalyptic prophecies, and visions of the Other World.

He: and you still have these texts?

I: of course! I had thought of bringing them with me but I wasn't sure I'd find you here.

He: do you remember if they bear the name of the author?

I: they're unsigned! The sender claims to be an old friend of yours in whose home you stayed during the last International Congress of Comparative Literature, just before the beginning of the siege. He would like to know your opinion of the "Dreams" and of a collection of poems that he apparently gave you as a gift during his visit. The title of it is doubtless an allusion to Sotades, the Greek bard who celebrated the sodality of sodomites, if you'll excuse the play on words!

He: *Sotadic Zone?*

I: exactly!

A sharp-edged silence suddenly cut off all conversation. Had I mentioned rope in the house of a hanged man? My colleague choked and had to be brought a glass of water; it allowed him to recover his breath, but it did not bring him out of a tense, stubborn muteness. As for his friend, the chronicler of Ben Sidi Abu al-Makârim, he slipped away without even saying good-bye: we thought he was in the toilet, until the owner of the little café explained to us that after paying the bill for everyone, he had disappeared in the nocturnal darkness of the empty, unlit streets.

E.

In the beginning, the impression that we had mastered the rules of the game that was meant to erase every trace of having whisked Ben Sidi Abu al-Makârim away and left the pseudo J. G. in his place—so as to disorient the Spanish major and draw him into quicksand that would swallow him up—made my colleague and me feel altogether satisfied. Victims of the cruelty of history, we took vengeance on it with our histories, woven out of ambiguities, interpolated texts, fabricated events: such is the marvelous power of literature. We had caused the representative of the multinational command, whose duplicitous language and cynicism had contributed to perpetuating our misfortunes, to lose his way in the labyrinth or garden of texts that fork and branch until eventually they weave a dense forest. Once he had played the role that we had spitefully assigned him, the disoriented major had been shipwrecked like a boat adrift until he lost his senses and ceased all activity. His having been put on sick leave for delirium or some mental ailment was a relief to everyone: his annoying and useless presence was a nuisance to us. The interpreters and prompters of our drama had no further need of him.

My friend and colleague's idea of introducing the collection of "J. G.'s" poems and his own stories into the plot we had invented, although an excellent one on first sight, nonetheless contained the premises of a series of geological faults and seismic jolts which, as I immediately realized, raised doubts as to how well founded my research and writings about Sidi Abu al-Makârim were. If some of the latter's poems appear to be in perfect harmony with my intuitive reconstruction of them, others are manifestly incompatible and belie his paternity. Even more serious than the already mentioned "Full Stop" and the anachronistic reference to Plautus and *La Celestina* was a mystico-erotic composition, with a long Latin epigraph, whose opening verses threatened to ruin my whole scheme:

Woodcutters, masons, guards, soldiers, wrestlers, brutish sons of
   the Sotadic zone.
I leaf through the album of the blurred, faded snapshots of you.

How could the real or the pseudo Ben Sidi Abu al-Makârim
refer to the poems of "J. G." and appropriate his carefully anno-
tated *Sotadic Zone?* The leaves of the notebook fell from my
hands like those of a tree in autumn. What would my friend, the
one who had been given the manuscript bought at the junk
dealer's stall, say when he saw these verses? The very thought of
how he would ridicule me and my holy man made me squirm,
and I decided to take drastic action: censor the poem, lock it up
in a drawer in my dark and dilapidated apartment. All at once, I
discovered that I had not mastered the rules of the game, that
they escaped me, that someone else—who?—was playing with
me as I had played with the major. The sensation of being spied
on from behind my back and manipulated at a distance robbed
me of autonomy, significance, and credibility. If I was nothing
but another of the multiple threads of the plot, who was playing
the principal role?

The appearance of D. K., the secretary of the Jewish Humanitarian, Cultural, and Educational Association, at the meeting of
the circle of polyglots was the final blow. My laborious reconstruction of the life and works of the obscure holy man of the
Maghreb included the mention of his frequent practice of humility that took the form of defecating in public and lo and be-
hold, the messiah or haranguer of the crowd in the metro in my
friend's stories inspired directly by him—a debt recognized in
writing in a note that he managed to send me—turned up
again, his buttocks spread, in one of the anonymous "Dreams"
delivered to D. K. by S. O. S. Sepharad!

I fled immediately from the polyglots' meeting, afraid I
would be the object of jeers and embarrassing questions, and
took refuge in the crypt of the hotel. I told my troubles to my
sister-in-law, who helped me out with the accounting and at the

reception desk, and she took advantage of the occasion to tell me what she thought of my colleague, criticizing, for good reason, his misogyny and in particular his malicious reference in his first narrative to the "grim and glassy look" in her eyes, inasmuch as she was especially proud of her calm, soft gaze that entrances everyone around her. His role in the affair, she maintained, had been of no use whatsoever and had caused nothing but confusion and complications. Just as he used your research concerning the holy man to invent the figure of the Defecator, she said, he's now going to take advantage of the mess he's gotten you into to dream up a new story that makes you look muddleheaded and credulous!

I let her go on ranting and raving about him and his mania for writing anything and everything, with reality and fantasy all jumbled together, and went up to the fifth floor to examine the debris of room 435, now swept into a pile in the corner.

I was vaguely hoping for a miracle—the reincarnation or theophany of the person who had disappeared—but to my great disappointment, this time Ben Sidi Abu al-Makârim did not show up at the rendezvous.

F.

The revelations and incidents that shook the foundations of the polyglot circle culminated in one last decisive calamity. For some time various members of the presidency and government had been regularly denouncing to the high command of the International Mediation Force the tactics of certain members of the military who were experts at all sorts of trafficking: abusing their prerogative as arbitrators, they engaged in the smuggling of alcohol, cigarettes, and drugs and the sale of icons and altarpieces, working hand and glove with the local mafia. A handful of men from the Ukrainian contingent stood out for their skill and brazenness in carving out a bright future for themselves at the expense of the 300,000 innocents trapped like rats in the city: that manhunt on a grand scale, filmed daily, with its shells, grenades, and snipers' bullets that the so-called negotiators from the UN and the EC described as a "fight between factions" and "tribal warfare"!

Among the objects sold at street stalls along the run-down and impoverished Avenue de la Marshal, manuscripts saved from the fire at the library as well as rare books of incalculable value had appeared; smuggled to countries that turn their backs on us today and close their eyes to the enormity of the crime committed against us, these treasures command phenomenally high prices in the hands of collectors and book dealers devoid of any sense of ethics and honor. Although these shady transactions all happen in broad daylight, police raids are helpless to stop them: their informers, past masters at double-dealing, tell the street vendors in advance what day and what time the police will be arriving.

Early in spring, when the besieged emerged en masse from their refuges and lairs to get a bit of fresh air and enjoy the mild weather of the season, late in coming that year, without fear of the habitual rain of shells fired down at them from the mountains, a writer with no talent who occasionally attended the meetings of the little circle of polyglots turned up unexpectedly at one of their gatherings, with an enigmatic smile on his face and badly overweight still despite his having lost more than thirty kilos during the siege. After greeting those present, he proudly set his worn leather briefcase down on the table. Renowned for his retractile tongue and his gift for malicious gossip, he admits to a mortal hatred of our old acquaintance, the narrator and Hispanicist, the author of the stories inserted in the first part of the book: eaten up with envy, he never misses an opportunity to criticize him and question his probity and talent. With the self-assurance of a card player hiding the winning ace up his sleeve, he took advantage of a pause in the conversation of those present and cleared his throat.

Well, then, he began by saying, I was out for a walk early this morning so as to take advantage of this pleasant bit of sunshine bestowing its warmth on us today, when I took it into my head to stroll by the secondhand book stalls and junk dealers' stands, and imagine my surprise when I suddenly came across several most interesting notebooks that I hastened to buy for just two marks!

(He opened the leather briefcase and waited a few seconds before staring our narrator in the face, with the eye of an expert sharpshooter aiming directly at his target.)

An uncensored copy of the collection of poems by "J. G." and five stories by my cherished friend and old traveling companion, which, according to the owner of the stall, he had acquired at the liquidation sale of the effects of a former leader of the International Mediation Force! Stories which, to judge from a quick first reading, offer certain curious variants of the original, unless (and here his smile spread out over his entire face, giving it an expression of feigned affability), unless, I repeat, the contrary is true: that this is the original and our friend's text is simply the work of a copyist, a plagiarism without the least trace of inspiration! Inasmuch as a line-by-line comparison of the two texts would be long and boring, I leave to you the honor of assembling a tribunal of ethical experts, charged with settling the question of the stories and pillorying their forger!

The spoilsport said good-bye with that gaping smile half detached from his lips and sliding down the corners of his mouth, mingled with a slaver of satisfaction: he knew that his contribution to the conversation had been a mortal blow to the members of the little circle and had put an end to their disquisitions regarding the paternity of the poems, that chain of uncertainties and suspicions that had gradually undermined their existence and plunged them into unreality.

Our two old friends and their colleagues sat there stunned, unable to face this new challenge, and someone brought up, to everyone's relief, one of Voltaire's short stories.

Do you remember that passage in *Candide* in which four or five dethroned kings happen to meet at an inn in a far-off country, each of them unaware of the hidden royalty of the others? During a lively game of cards they discover their amazing kinship and each of them marvels in turn at their extraordinary meeting! Well, what's happening to us is very much like that! Isn't it unbelievable, but true, that we are at once investigators, storytellers, poets, forgers, and manipulators of texts? How to explain rationally this series of coincidences except by the fact that, victims of a siege that a few years back we would have considered unthinkable, we have turned into characters of a history forced upon us? The lords of war and their accomplices are writing the script and manipulating us like puppets from their vantage point high above us! Reality has been transmuted into fiction: the horror tale of our daily existence!

The explosion very close by of a mortar shell that fortunately left no victims—fired "accidentally" by the aggressors according to the usual version put out by the multinational command—scattered the members of the polyglot circle: like nocturnal insects surprised by the intrusion of a light, they ran to take shelter in their refuges and never met together again.

IV. OPEN LETTER FROM THE MAJOR TO THE ADMINISTRATORS OF THE MILITARY PSYCHIATRIC CENTER

In circumstances such as these—I am referring to the privation of my freedom to which I find myself subjected for weeks now—the frame of mind of the supposed patient, confronted simultaneously with himself and with the limits imposed by the medical authorities, leads him, with no need for collaboration with anyone else, to rake over the ashes of his past again and again in search of answers to and clarifications of the questions that he keeps asking himself.

Since being put on sick leave by the the International Mediation Force, transferred to the allied military base at A. and hospitalized at the psychiatric center of N. which is under the jurisdiction of the Ministry of Defense, I have lived in a state of regression, vividly reliving episodes of my childhood and family scenes that I believed to be forever buried. It is as if a seismic cataclysm had violently jolted the hidden strata of my life and caused them to rise to the surface, thereby facilitating my work as an archaeologist. The ruins of a country and a home that were victims of a bloody fratricidal war are now in full view: eloquent, accusatory wounds, not yet healed over. In the grip of commingled sadness and indignation, I wander obsessively among those ruins.

Born in 1946, in the military garrison of T., I lived there for approximately ten years until the sudden independence of the country and the abandonment of our Protectorate. A tranquil childhood in a traditional military milieu, a strict religious and patriotic education in classrooms presided over by a crucifix and portraits of the Generalísimo and the founder of the Falangist party. My father sometimes took me to the barracks of the regiment in which he served, and I remember having watched, saluting with him from the reviewing stand, troops parading by: legionnaires, native infantrymen, soldiers of the regular army, all those whose courage and abnegation had contributed to the triumph of "the Crusade." My career was laid out for me in advance, without my advice or consent: I would be an army officer, following the tradition in my father's family;

once I had my diploma from secondary school, I would enter the Military Academy.

My mother had been a woman of great beauty: cultured, refined, a voracious reader of novels and poetry, she did not spend time with the wives of the other junior and senior officers or attend their social gatherings or charity benefits. Later on, I heard it rumored that these ladies attributed her secluded life to my father's jealousy and possessiveness. Today I am inclined to believe that she imposed this semicloistered existence on herself. Married for reasons unknown to me to a man with a background and tastes that couldn't have been more different from her own, she had managed to preserve, thanks to her gentleness and patience, a small portion of independence in the prudish and unrefined world of of the military caste serving in Africa. Books and the rearing of her only son— two other brothers of mine had died within a few days of their birth before I came into the world—occupied her days sufficiently to keep her from ever being bored. The ideal world of her hours spent reading and her time alone with me were her secret garden: I was the only one allowed to enter it.

Although I still have only a handful of photographs of her in the spacious villa we lived in at the foot of the mountain, I remember her look of joy as she took me in her arms to welcome me when I came home on holiday from the religious brothers' school to which I was sent. When I was with her, I sensed the existence of a world to which, to my misfortune, I was never to have access: that of a culture, a sensitivity and feelings carefully banished from the classrooms at school. When my father joined us, order imposed from the outside ruled the day. But my furtive forays into her study were no doubt the most luminous moments of my childhood.

It was there, in that room whose walls were lined with books, that I heard my mother utter for the first time, in the course of a conversation with one of her cousins who had come from the Peninsula on a visit, the name of my uncle Eusebio. The two of them were whispering so that I wouldn't overhear them, and my mother began to cry. I must have asked her why, for she dried her tears, attributing them to the heat. Later, as I pretended to be asleep on the little sofa in the study, I collected the scattered seeds of her confidences which, forty years afterward, during my temporary assignment to the high command of the International Mediation Force, suddenly germinated in my consciousness. Phrases, bits of sentences, spoken first by her and then by my father, in the study, or perhaps in their bedroom or in the drawing room: allusions to Uncle Eusebio's detention on the day of the Uprising, the threat of summary proceedings, I knelt at his feet, I pleaded and pleaded like a madwoman, only your intervention can save him, if they take him away to be shot it will be as if they were taking me away, I always told you he'd come to a bad end, a Red, a poet, and a queer, do you realize? do it for me, for the love of God! think of the shame and dishonor for the family! What happened to Uncle Eusebio, I asked her days later when, nestling on her bosom, I was enjoying with her the quiet and the magic of her refuge. Your father saved him from the firing squad and they shut him up in an insane asylum that he later escaped from; he proved that he was a man of his word, it was an act of great courage in those circumstance, for which I am grateful to him and will be grateful for the rest of my life. But don't repeat a word of what I just told you to anyone, keep it all a secret between just the two of us, don't mention the name of my brother in front of him, he'd be beside himself, he'd never forgive me! The past is over and done with. Put what happened out of your mind!

She never again mentioned the subject in her rare and invariably discreet confidences, not even in her last days in the hospital, when the illness that was undermining her from within took her to her grave at last. At the time I was already a grown man and had blocked out and buried deep within myself the conversation about my uncle and another disturbing incident that also happened in T.

It was in the heat of summer. My parents had gone out and I

took advantage of their absence to steal into my mother's refuge; I searched about for the tiny keys to the richly decorated cabinet with little drawers that was the finest piece of furniture that she had brought in her dowry and the one in which she kept her correspondence with the family and her husband's love letters. One by one, I opened all its compartments until I came across an envelope with a wax seal hidden in the gap between the boards of the little bottom drawer. Written on the envelope were the few concise words: "Given to my sister on July 17, 1936, with the request that she destroy it in case of my death or disappearance." Did I really open it? Or is the whole thing a later mental construction? Although the psychiatrist with whom I discuss the subject adamantly argues, in his intolerable Freudian (or Lacanian?) jargon, in favor of the second hypothesis, I relive the scene with a clarity and an exactness of detail that belies his theories and elucubrations. The language of psychoanalysts has always seemed to me to be schematic and false: the pretension of fitting the experiences lived by the person who, in my case, is not so much a patient as an "impatient" into a prefabricated conceptual mold is as vain an undertaking as trying to collect water in a fishnet. What is buried and fraught with meaning will inevitably escape through the meshes.

Inside the envelope—what became of it later on? —was a notebook containing poems, letters, and photographs. I have no clear memory of the notebook, but I can describe the photographs and missives in detail. The latter were undoubtedly written by near illiterates—in a crude, phonetic approximation of proper Spanish—illustrated at times with obscene sketches: stiff penises, crudely drawn, in the act of urinating or spurting semen. The yellowed, faded snapshots were clumsy portraits of strong, husky lads, Moroccan infantrymen or soldiers in the regular army, sporting mustaches, in uniform, their flies open, proudly showing off the size and vigor of their attributes, their natural weapon at the ready. I closed the envelope, put it back in its hiding place, and ran to the toilet, to masturbate or to vomit, I don't remember which.

I buried the incident in the most profound forgetfulness possible and took up the career I was destined for in advance by the circumstances in which my childhood and education had unfolded: brilliant studies at the Military Academy, marriage to a woman with whom I had two children, assignments to various barracks in the Peninsula, language courses and special training in Texas, liaison officer to allied headquarters during the Gulf War, appointment as commissioner for civil affairs attached to the high command of the International Mediation Force in S. in fall 1993. There my past caught up with me in the form of a death with no corpse: a compatriot hit by a mortar shell in his room at the hotel H. I., whose notebook of poems brought back the memory of my uncle Eusebio. The supposed initials of its author were not the same as his; but in those days—that terrible summer of 1936—the survival instinct strongly counseled caution. Verses like those could bring their author before a firing squad, with a bullet in the ass for good measure, as happened to the poet from Granada. With one difference: at the fort of M.— the bastion of the military personnel who had taken part in the Uprising—the repression of nonconformists and dissidents was even more relentless.

At the risk of making my case look worse in the eyes of the doctors in charge of keeping my so-called schizophrenia under control, using methods that are no doubt gentler than those used to deal with my uncle Eusebio yet restrict my freedom and reduce me, morally speaking, to the status of a minus-value—a mere object of their analyses and conclusions—the experience of these weeks has breached many dams and opened the sluices to a flow of ideas held back for a period of forty years. Now that my blinders have fallen away, I see clearly that our role as observers attached to the International Mediation Force does not serve the cause of the victims but instead defends a status quo that favors the aggressors: that army of treacherous officers who in April 1992 trained their weapons on the people that they had sworn to defend, thus following in the footsteps of the hired assassins who staged an uprising in our country in '36 to save it from a "Judeo-Masonic conspiracy" and mercilessly crushed those who did not share their aims.

I do not know what fate holds in store for me after this violent jolt: my abrupt reencounter with the past will doubtless have lasting effects. I am left with only one certainty: if my personal situation permits, I will follow the example of my compatriot, the former United Nations high commissioner for refugees, who, after resigning with dignity from his post, has scathingly denounced the collusion between the negotiators or international cardsharps and the cynical and rapacious boss of Pale. Moreover, I do not dismiss the idea of getting back into uniform, not to patrol in the armored tanks of the International Mediation Force and show endless scruples and hesitations when it comes time to fix responsibilities when hundreds of grenades rain down from the mountains onto the hapless inhabitants of this rattrap of a city, but rather to enlist in the ranks of its defenders. Everything my mother put up with in silence rises today like a tide that threatens to drown me: my wish to survive morally forces me to side with dignity. Without the slightest romanticism, but simply to restore my ties with what I was cut off from in my childhood, I shall return to the banks of the Miljaka. There I shall perish or settle accounts once and for all with my mortal enemy.

V. FINAL DREAM

The editor has put you in charge of collecting the many texts and voices of the author or authors of the book, of putting together the scattered pieces of a puzzle that the members of his editorial committee have racked their brains to solve, only to finally throw in the towel. Only someone like yourself, an engineer and musician, he says, can reconcile the differences, link the disparate parts, weave together heterogeneous elements, avoid anachronisms and inconsistencies, reconstruct the overall architecture and design of that heap of sworn testimony, documents, narratives, poems that has piled up here on my office desk. Without your inspired hand, this *monstruum horrendum, informe, ingens* would become the butt of the critics' sarcasms and the public's rejection, ending up, despite its considerable weight and its pretensions, in the wastebasket!

Determined to show yourself equal to the challenge, you undertake the task of assembling the chapters by subject, of discovering its subtle links and connections of polishing its rough edges, of fitting them together with the aim of giving them an orderly structure or plot with a certain overall coherence. Patiently and carefully, you group together, parcel out, harmonize the voices of the chorus as a function of their affinities and divergences. Conscientiously, methodically, you endeavor to tie up loose ends, to eliminate little obtrusive loops and frayed edges that do not meet your standards as a skilled and experienced creator of textual canvases, without noticing that, when you tie one thread in, you loosen and undo the link with another, that as you weave and unweave, what you have gained one day is lost the next: every question that is resolved brings up more questions. You live in the middle of an Oriental tale: a painfully opened exit leads only to a closed door that on being forced open leads to yet another that will have to be broken down, and so on ad infinitum. Merely envisaging the situation discourages you and exhausts you. The entire undertaking is a trap: by accepting the editor's offer you've taken the bait and been hooked! Like Sisyphus, you will roll your rock uphill to the top of the mountain for all eternity!

Caught up in one of those nightmares in which the dreamer loses his way, has no idea how to find the path home, and instead of drawing ever closer, strays even farther from the place in the city where he lives, roams about amid forbidding landscapes, fords raging streams and rivers, scales steep slopes and mountainsides, his abode ever more distant, so you wander farther and farther afield from the book, from the urgent task of compiling the material at hand and making of it a conventional novel, a presentable, well-made market product. You have climbed snow-covered peaks, covered with birches and firs, and from this vantage point you observe, helplessly, the besieged city far below.

Have you perhaps taken advantage of the opening of a "tourist route," ironically suggested to you by a member of the polyglot circle thoroughly familiar with Swift's works, a route whereby those fond of powerful sensations would be able to journey without risk to the mountain heights that surround the rattrap and there enjoy the thrilling spectacle of its bombardment, with the right to participate in it if such were their inclination or desire?

As the fury of the artillerymen redoubles, you suddenly find yourself in the middle of the devastated area. Mutilated faces, spilled guts, wounds still oozing pus, horrifying scars; buildings that are burned-out shells, with nothing left of them but their framework, rusted carcasses, charred scaffolding, skeletons eaten away by urine; amputated stumps, dental prostheses, shattered tibiae, nasal cavities, inert jawbones, as though frozen in a rictus of terror. Snow covers the pile of bones beneath a charitable shroud. Those who live in the neighborhood remain cloistered in their little cells and there is not a living soul to be seen.

You run, you zigzag, trying to dodge the dangerous rain of shells and the practiced aim of the huntsmen. Hidden somewhere in the ruins a woman, a beautiful and eternally young mother, plays the piano: it's the Brahms sonata! You search about desperately for her in hostile, blackened buildings, in cellars, in dark refuges clustered together. Is there no one to hear this music? Are you the only one still alive, still palpitating, still trembling in this city that appears to be dead yet continues to be mercilessly pounded?

Anguish grips you, tightens its pincers, turns your heart into nothing but a mechanically ticking clock. A pendular movement accelerated by the proximity of the massive building painted yellow, hotel transformed into a crypt, sunlight reflecting off its countless ocelli, covered over with plastic: myriad simple eyes of a repugnant insect observed through a magnifying glass, with its legs, antennae, tarsi, thorax, womb of your dreams and your visions of horror. Is someone crouched down spying on you through a peephole punched open in one of the blind windows? Is he watching, as you are, the most feared scene of all, repeated endlessly?

A long sidewalk carpeted in white, an ordinary wall a meter high running alongside what remains of a park with meticulously pruned trees, the silhouette of a woman dressed in a dark winter coat, her head covered with a black kerchief. A body lying facedown on the ground, exhausted from its Via Crucis on its knees to the protective carcass that was once the state museum? Its prolonged immobility points to an infinitely harsher reality. The bullet has gone through her neck, blood is running out and dyeing the snow red. The past is being repeated and reprinted in the present: no one escapes fate and its natural cruelty. The delicate hands clutching the bag exist only in your mind. You do not need to open it to know what is inside. You will never hear the notes being played on the piano again.

APPENDIX

I. *SOTADIC ZONE*

During so many empty hours with no support
(without a ray of light transpiercing me)
I call to mind the lineaments of that coarse uniform, the humble
    veil of your robust attributes.

Immediate fusion, submission of my body to your patient
    craftsmanship
tentatively, intermittently, until it is centered on the nucleus or
    precise place of torment and pleasure.

Shaped by your broad, hard, rigorous hands, made to knead, mold,
    give human form to a malleable lump of clay
(creating me, expertly and carefully, as you would a bowl or jar)
you are my potter.

You calm and excite, you alternate currents, you accentuate the
    pressure of your palms, pour over me your thick, swirling
    slip, explore with greedy lips, searing volcano, abyss that
    sucks me in!
I am your creature.

Where do you wander, soul, in those moments of fulfillment and
    delight?
Do you inspire the manual ardor that flares up in my breast?
    or the urgent tightening of the rough barbs?
(patch of scrub, thicket of blinding blackness).

Do you steal away from the rendezvous?
or do you witness, hidden behind your veil, with embarrassment
    and dismay, the accelerated pulsing of my member as it
    blindly broadcasts its infertile seed?

                                                    (*The Potter*)

Save from oblivion the hard-won images of his luminous
        nocturnal appearance
boots, pants, beret, shoulder braid, shirt
opulent, promising, armed trousers fly
heavy belt at his waist with its long, dangling *zeruata*
(emblem or complement to the other one
ready to frisk and frolic behind the cloth, palpitating as you
        palpate it).

Render homage to the two of them in turn
(the real truncheon and its swollen symbol)
until the hammerlock embrace, devouring pleasure, imbricated
        entwining!

Brief visits, their clarity grown musty and faded in the mad haste
of the passsing days.

Were they visions or precise highlights of a superior reality?

Their brightness did not last beyond the writing.

                                        (*The Body Guard*)

In reality or in dreams
or re-creating it still in my minute hand.

Rock crystal, rocky crystallization, refraction, impenetrability.

Vast curved torso, sturdy overlapping of robust muscles
massive skull, rough, weathered face, handlebar mustache, ends
      curving upward
(handlebar or coiled whip)

marks, bare scars of a burly brute, a veteran wrestler.

Invested with the power and majesty of your scepter
(stout, labiate club, its extreme fervor never declining)
you officiate in all your trappings, silent liturgy of communion
(idol, stud stallion, haughty guard).

Giver, the gesture threatening
(raise your nail-studded leather wristband if your authority is still
      unquestioned)
you contemplate the adorer from above
(estranged from or alien to the pleasure you dispense behind the
      inscrutable opacity of your dark glasses)
the being humbly prostrated, absorbed in his exercises of
      devotion.

How to halt the flight of time?

Vertigo of immobility
respected rigor
consummation of the rite.
Awaiting the tense syncopated virtue
lustral bath or abundant spring of your disdain spilled out.

                                           (*Mystery Play*)

Impossible to encompass his great chest.

You gain access to him from the side, you make your way into
the hirsute foliage
Shade, undergrowth, brush.

Fleece rough and untamed.

Thickets easy to go astray in.

Hillocks hidden in the bush.

All uncultivated, left fallow.

(*Silviculturist*)

Bulbs
the stem erect, fungiform
topped with a cap or blood-gorged crown.

Genetic splendor.

Vigor, spurt of sperm, fecundation.

Perplexity
(scourge of saints)

Wide gullets or truth hard to swallow?

(*Guide to the Perplexed*)

You gobble down the baited hook
(promise of bitterness)

You take communion blindly.

Before you, back gracefully arched
the ever-repeated enigma.

(*Colophon*)

II. ASTROLABE

Is corporal violence a reflection of that of the universe?

Are we infinitesimal particles condemned to it by an unknown law
      or immanence?

How to subdue the inner fire if the glow of the furtive word does
      not enlighten us?

I grope for reasons for consolation.

I cling to the multiplicity of incidental things
(traps, trompe l'oeil)
that veil the essence of the One Being or make it seem to vanish.

                    (*Baraka of the Seal of the Saints*)

Is the cosmos generalized chaos since its unheard initial
   explosion?

Otherwise how to explain the attractions, repulsions, centrifugal
   forces, astral collisions, black holes, devouring abysses?

Does our microscopic history ceaselessly reproduce the sound
   and the fury, the disillusioned maxim of Plautus, Petrarchian
   pessimism, and the cruel world of *La Celestina*?

*(what more terrrible war than to engender in your body the one who
will gnaw away your vitals?)*

Lord of Violence

if you created us to live in perpetual contention

in what private heaven are you hiding the mantle of your mercy or
   rhama?

(Invocation)

You call to mind empires fallen to ruin, devastated dwellings, the
        slow decrepitude of corrupt people
everything they did while they lived and had power
what they achieved, how they went to perdition, how they were
        induced to rob and abuse those weaker than they
(their souls took wing, they were left soulless).

Although they may feel firmly established at the summit, in reality
        they are still journeying
their past does not exist
their present will disappear.

Where are those who preceded them in their thirst for power and
        riches?
in the end what did they earn for themselves in their lifetime?
what was their contribution to the light of humanity?

> (*Reading of the "Epistolarium" of Alí in the Patio of Sidí Bufdail*)

A fleeting glitter of images at the bottom of the abyss.

The grace of the Word transpierces you, illuminates you, takes you
back to your aridities.

Swift flashes, barely set alight before they are extinguished, cause
of abjection and perplexity.

Opacity, unsureness, brevity of the gift.

You leaf through, listlessly, sterile pages of your dictionary.

(*Candelabrum for Tenebrae*)

Woodcutters, masons, guards, soldiers, wrestlers, brutish sons of
    the Sotadic zone.
I leaf through the album of the blurred, faded snapshots of you.

Are you still alive, confined as I am to a disagreeable old age, to
    the heat of your native land, home and family?

(the collusion of cheap hotels and *alhamas* forgotten)
    or have you been swept away by a puff of wind, with your
    leathery vigor and appetite for life?

(do plants with powerful sap feed on them? or is their
    decomposition vain and unproductive?)

If I call to mind your magnanimity and shared immediacy I do not
    do so out of vainglory or senile nostalgia.

I uphold

(against all evidence)

the resurrection.

There is a promise of intoxication beyond the ephemeral
    appearance of things.

      (*Quod resurrectio futura non debet concedi a philosopho, quia
      impossibilium est eam investigari per rationem*)

From the I to the I
the distance is immense.

A rope stretched across the void.

How to bring the extremes together
how to compile the infinite dispersion of a life?

Broken memory, vespertine light.
Raw material or sign?

(*Momentary Flows*)

In your mad race against time
(few grains of sand are now left in the top of the hourglass)
you devote yourself to more and more travels, escapes, advances,
orgasms, dangers.

In search of the bullet that will mow you down?
or of a writing that also escapes you and slips between your
fingers?

Death and decrepitude are everywhere around you.
How to avoid erosion with dignity?

(Full Stop)